STELLA IN HEAVEN

G·K
Hall
&Co.

Also by Art Buchwald
in Large Print:

I'll Always Have Paris!
Leaving Home
Lighten Up, George
Whose Rose Garden Is It Anyway?
I Think I Don't Remember
"You Can Fool All of the People
   All of the Time"
While Reagan Slept

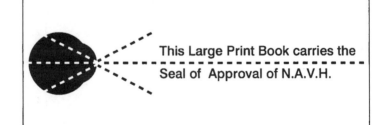

This Large Print Book carries the
Seal of Approval of N.A.V.H.

STELLA IN HEAVEN

Art Buchwald

G.K. Hall • Thorndike, Maine

Published in 2001 by arrangement with G. P. Putnam's Sons,
a member of Penguin Putnam Inc.

G.K. Hall Large Print Core Series.

The text of this Large Print edition is unabridged.
Other aspects of the book may vary from the original edition.

Set in 16 pt. Plantin by Susan Guthrie.

Printed in the United States on permanent paper.

Library of Congress Cataloging-in-Publication Data
Buchwald, Art.
   Stella in heaven : almost a novel / Art Buchwald.   LP
     p.   cm.
   ISBN 0-7838-9308-6 (lg. print : hc : alk. paper)
   1. Spouses — Death — Psychological aspects — Fiction.
  2.Widowers — Fiction.   3. Large type books. I. Title.
  PS3503.U1828 S7 2000b
  813′.54—dc21
                                      00-046194

Thanks to Carol Rial, Phyllis Grann,
and Stacy Creamer

Roger's Story

My name is Roger Folger, I'm sixty-one years old, and I'm a widower. My wife, Stella, went to Heaven two years ago at the age of fifty-nine, mainly, Dr. Rappaport said, from consuming a pack of cigarettes a day.

I was married to Stella for thirty-eight years and like most marriages, some of it was good and some of it was not perfect. I'm afraid she might say the same thing or something different.

What I didn't expect is that she would go to Heaven before me. I was crazy enough to think I could decide who died first. But it was Stella who made the decisions in the family, including this one. She was the strong one in the family and everyone had to follow her. She decided where we went on vacation, what movie we were going to see, when we went out for dinner and when we stayed home. The kids called her "Mrs. McNamara, the leader of the band."

In my immediate family Stella left behind my forty-year-old son, Timmy, who works with poor kids in the Bronx, and my thirty-eight-year-old daughter, Sarah, who can be a bit of a problem. Sarah still lives at home with me and my mother, Mimi, who drove Stella crazy throughout our marriage.

Do I miss Stella? The answer is very much. I'm

very lonely without her. The only thing that makes it at all livable is that I talk to her every night. I know it sounds crazy, but we converse without any problem, she in Heaven, I in my bedroom. We've been doing it ever since she passed away. How it got started is that a week after she was buried I went to the cemetery to put flowers on her grave and said how much I missed her. All of a sudden I heard her voice.

"Roger! It's me and the Divine Telephone Service — and it's free!"

"Stella! Does this mean we can talk to each other every day?"

"Of course. I've got a Princess phone right in my room."

I was thrilled. It was almost like being married again.

So all of a sudden we were right back to our chats, and our disagreements. With us it's not always "I love you" and "Wish you were here."

For example, one night a few weeks ago Stella told me Mrs. Gittleson, who lived on 63rd Road, passed away. Mrs. Gittleson told Stella that I had become the Don Juan of Forest Hills and had been dating a different lady every week.

This got me very angry and I told Stella that Mrs. Gittleson was a bitch on Earth and she's a bitch now. I also asked what she was doing in Heaven in the first place.

Stella said, "You shouldn't talk that way about the dead."

I didn't want to defend myself but I felt I had

to. I explained to Stella that I didn't go out with any one woman because I didn't want to get into a serious relationship. As a matter of fact, I didn't know what I wanted. I took one lady to the movies, another to the theater, one to dinner and someone else to watch the Mets.

But I didn't shimmy between the sheets with any of them.

Of course, Stella wanted to know if I desired to. I said that I didn't and neither did they.

Before we go any further, let me say that I'm not a swinger. You could call me an average person who would have remained a loyal husband if his wife hadn't died.

I was born and raised in Montclair, New Jersey, the only son of a domineering mother and a drunk father. My mother tried to remain in complete charge of my life, even after I got married. My father was a certifiable alcoholic and our basement was piled high with empty liquor bottles. He insisted on saving every empty bottle of liquor he consumed. He said each bottle reminded him of a memorable time he had without my mother.

My mother came from Hungarian stock. My grandparents were from Budapest. They settled in the Bronx, where my grandfather worked for a tailor. My grandmother was even more outspoken than my mother. Every time someone did something she didn't like, she put a curse on them. My mother explained to me that even if it wasn't a real curse, it was enough of one to frighten the other person, so it served its purpose. Everyone called my grandmother "Big Mimi" and my mother "Little Mimi."

As the only child, I was Little Mimi's pride and joy. To make sure I didn't do anything wrong, she searched my room once a week. One time she found a Trojan rubber at the bottom of a drawer. I told her I was just keeping it for a latex experiment in chemistry class, but she was furious and spanked my bottom as hard as she could.

My father died when I was ten years old. I guess I was sorry to see him go, but he wasn't much of a father. Because of his inebriation I could never understand a word he said.

Mimi went through a grieving process when he died, but it didn't last very long. In fact, within six months she confessed to me that she had made a mistake when she married him. She told me that my father wasn't what she'd bargained for and if she had to do it all over, she would never marry anyone unless he drove a new Pontiac.

My school life was no better or worse than anyone else's who grew up in Montclair. Mimi had a job as a nurse and I was left alone to amuse myself.

My best friend was Twoey McGowan and he's still my best friend today. Twoey is Irish and has red hair and freckles all over. He told me he got the name Twoey because he was the second one born in his family. He didn't mind the name but no one ever spelled it right.

Twoey and I were inseparable. We went downtown every day hoping to find stuff that might have fallen out of someone's shopping bag. We'd go into a Montgomery Ward's and he'd start screaming and holding his groin. While he had everyone's attention, I'd grab whatever was on the counter. It never failed.

At thirteen Twoey also told me how to French-kiss. He said French-kissing was God's way of telling women they should have children.

Sex was constantly on our minds. We once went up to Twoey's apartment and watched through a window across the street while a young woman disrobed to take a bath. She had flaming blonde hair and great, round breasts. The next night we looked again, and a male the size of a grizzly bear was in the room, scratching his hairy stomach. He suddenly saw us and started yelling and flailing his arms around. We jumped down and pulled the blinds closed, hoping Mimi hadn't heard him.

While somewhat mischievous, I was good in school and got A's most of the time. Mimi wouldn't accept anything less. Early on I told her I wanted to be a scientist. She said that was a mistake because scientists, unlike lawyers, couldn't charge by the hour. But she didn't fight me when the A's rolled in.

Twoey, on the other hand, earned C's and D's. He said it didn't bother him because he was going to become a builder when he grew up, and

11

you didn't need good grades to build houses.

Stella's Story

I'm Stella, the deceased. I'm in Heaven just like the song says. I'm happy here, though it doesn't mean I wouldn't be happier on Earth. My family and friends are there and I miss them very much.

So what is Heaven like? The only thing I can compare it to is the Ritz-Carlton in Florida. Roger and I celebrated our 25th Anniversary there, in a suite overlooking the Gulf of Mexico. Up here almost everyone has a suite with an ocean view. The lobby is decorated with the finest French and English furniture and has art to die for. They have everything from Leonardo da Vinci to Norman Rockwell.

Our Heaven is managed by Moses and St. Peter is the assistant manager. No one ever sees God. Like all Ritz-Carltons, the manager hangs out behind a closed door in the back.

You have to follow certain rules. You have to keep the noise down, which makes life difficult for people from New York. You're not supposed to cry or complain and, above all, you have to love your neighbor even if you're not certain about her. Some people can't take the lack of conflict so there is a free shuttle bus that runs on the hour and will take them to you-know-where.

The lobby is covered in gold. Two angels

manage the reception desk and check you in when you first arrive. The concierge is Mary Magdalene and her friendly staff is there to take care of all your needs, and the bellman will do anything for you but he won't take tips. You are not permitted to tip here at all, which is how you know this is truly Heaven.

What makes it especially relaxing is that you can order up a massage anytime you want, so you're always relaxed in the evening when Mozart gives a recital.

Roger once asked if I had enough to do in Heaven.

I told him everything is available. There are cooking lessons with the greatest chefs in the world. You can either get tailored clothes or Ralph Lauren off the rack for free. We have lectures by everyone from Maimonides to Winston Churchill. My favorite speaker is Franklin D. Roosevelt. When he tells us how we got involved in World War II, it's riveting. Everyone loves to listen to Eleanor too. When the Roosevelts come over from wherever they're staying in Heaven, it's standing room only.

You can have room service here anytime you want and you can order up everything you desire, including chocolate fudge sundaes and crepes suzette — without getting fat.

I have a beautiful living room with Louis the XIVth furniture, where I can entertain my friends, and a lovely bedroom with a Marie Antoinette bed.

Roger asked me if we have television.

"No," I said, "Moses won't allow it. It's full of violence and wife-beating. He told us, 'If you want television, go to Hades.' "

We can see movies like *Casablanca*, *Gone With the Wind* and the Marx Brothers, but Moses won't allow gangster movies with James Cagney or Edward G. Robinson. He also won't show *The Godfather* because he says it portrays human beings in a very bad light.

One of the things available to us is concerts by the greatest musicians who ever lived. I saw Beethoven sitting in a box the other night while Leonard Bernstein was conducting the Ninth Symphony. He seemed to approve. And people who are interested in art can take courses from Michelangelo and Andy Warhol.

You're probably wondering if there's anyone up here who shouldn't be here. Some of us think so, but we don't want to say anything because it might get back to Moses that we're criticizing the clientele. I heard there was some discussion over whether Picasso should have come to Heaven since he had such a wild life on Earth, but it was decided he was such a genius that, if rejected, he would wind up painting for the Devil. So he's around here too.

Moses encourages people to get involved in sports too. We have an Olympic-sized swimming pool, a soccer field, a basketball court and a completely furnished gym. We don't compete because this causes ill feelings. Everyone competes against himself. There is a salon where you can play bridge, a ski lift outside the door, a bridle path, a bowling alley and a spa. You can also play golf where the course is designed so that you never hit a bad shot. There are also tennis courts and croquet greens. If you ask for a sport and they don't have it, they'll get it for you.

What makes Heaven really Heaven for women is that they don't have to dust or vacuum or do the dishes. Roger asked me who did those chores and I told him nothing ever gets dirty.

"Is there a temple up there?" he once asked me.

I told him there's any house of worship you could ask for. But there is a rule which is strictly observed. No one can make fun of anybody else's religion. You can worship any God you want but you can't interfere with somebody else's beliefs. If you do, they will kick you out.

"Is this Moses' rule?"

"It's God's. He really has a thing about everyone claiming their religion is the only one. He gave Moses strict instructions that if anyone tried to cause trouble, he's to pull the trap door."

"So being Jewish doesn't make you any better or any worse than anybody else?"

"Right, but you can practice any religion. They even have a kosher kitchen if you want. The thing is Catholics, Jews, Protestants, Muslims, Buddhists and Hindus get along just fine. Besides, when everything is great, there's no reason to think that one of the other religions is going to hurt you."

I hate to say this but not everyone in Heaven is an angel. As a matter of fact, not every angel in Heaven is an angel. There is one angel named Prudin who is a real pain in the neck. She's into everybody's business and is constantly reporting misdemeanors to Moses. He doesn't like the idea, but angels have a different status than the rest of us. They can't be kicked out and they can only be punished by God.

Rumor has it that Prudin was up for sainthood but when her name came up in the Vatican, she was unanimously voted down because no matter what she did for the poor she wanted everyone to know about it.

They say that when Prudin asked a friend in Rome, "Was I blackballed by one priest or two?" the friend said, "Have you ever seen caviar?"

I don't know if she's bitter because she didn't make sainthood or if she's just a troublemaker.

Roger's Story

Let me explain what is going on with me. I didn't pick the role of widower. It was thrust on me by fate or God or the tobacco companies. For me it's a lousy role because after being married so long, I have no experience in life management.

I didn't know what it was going to be like to be

16

a widower. My men friends think it's a snap. The first realization I had that it wasn't easy was when I discovered the dirty shirts had started piling up and I didn't know where the laundry was. Then I didn't know where the dry cleaner was. Every chore around the house had been done by Stella. And when she left me, I'd never been so frightened in my life.

During our married life Stella made all the family decisions at home and I made all the decisions in the lab, where I've been working on a cure for herpes for the last thirty years. She was Queen Elizabeth and I, Prince Philip.

People believe that a widower is a swinger and as soon as his wife passes away he's making whoopee with every woman in New York City. If I take a woman to lunch from the lab, the tom-toms immediately start beating that I'm seeing her.

If you were to ask me what I've been doing for pleasure since I've become a widower, I'd tell you that I've become a do-gooder. I find myself spending a lot of energy on getting people out of trouble. When I was married trouble was something people dealt with in their own lives. But now that I'm single, people consider me a life-line. Getting involved in other people's lives is something I would never have thought of doing when Stella was alive.

A recent example is when an assistant in my lab, Nelly Loughlin, came to work in hysterics. She had had a boyfriend named Tom who left her for another woman. Nelly, who was deeply in love with Tom, wrote him that she would die if he didn't come back. She also had an ex-husband who somehow got a hold of the letter, took it to a judge and said his ex-wife was suicidal and their ten-year-old daughter was not safe. The judge agreed and gave the girl to the father.

I got involved, something Stella never would have let me do. We hired a lawyer and then a psychiatrist to prove she wasn't suicidal. We also heard through the grapevine that the ex-husband was involved in vice. I called Twoey and told him the story. He said he knew a private detective who owed him a favor. We put him on the case. He discovered the ex-husband was a male prostitute who ran ads in Greenwich Village sex newspapers. I told Twoey we should take the information to the judge, but he had a better idea. The private eye, Twoey and I paid a visit to the ex in Jackson Heights, produced the ads and told him he had five minutes to give the kid back or we were going to take the story to the *New York Post*. And we all know what they would do with it.

So the ex-husband saw our side of it and produced the little girl, whom we returned to the mother.

This is the kind of stuff widowers get involved with. Truth is, it makes me feel good that someone still needs me. Helping is an honorable profession but you can get more business than you can handle.

One of the main things that I don't like about being a widower is when people treat you differently. To some you are only good for filling a chair at a dinner party, and to some you are a poor soul to be patronized. To others you are just someone to be fixed up with somebody's friend. Hardly any of it is fun, and after a while you'd rather stay home.

Stella's Story

One of the things that makes Heaven Heaven is when you first arrive you are entitled to three wishes.

St. Peter wanted to know what my wish was and I said I wished to speak with Roger anytime I wanted to. It was granted and that is how we started talking in the cemetery. It has been a blessing. And I still have two wishes to go.

My best friend in Heaven is Bea Weinglass. She was fifty years old and divorced when she passed away two years ago, a victim of an automobile accident on the New Jersey Turnpike. It was a drunken driver and he hit her head on. Despite the accident, Bea is quite beautiful. In Heaven, no matter what happens to you on Earth, they make you look very good.

Bea's ex-husband was a snake. He tried to sue the drunken driver, but her brother, a lawyer, stepped in and said the insurance money belonged to Bea's children, Aldo and Henry. Bea's brother made a good case for the children by telling the ex-husband he'd smash his face in if he ever showed up in court.

I love Bea very much. She makes me laugh. Even in Heaven things can get ridiculous.

One time a beautiful woman in leotards came into the dining room. Bea went up to her and said, "If you hadn't died from high cholesterol, we'd kill you."

There is an old man here that Bea and I decided must have been rich because he keeps muttering to himself, "I should have taken it with me. I should have taken it with me."

Bea and I play Scrabble and one of us always comes up with good words that the other hadn't thought of.

We have lots of laughs. Even in Heaven you have to see the humor of things.

So far I've had a good time, although I have to say I miss Roger very much. We were married for a very long time and we're still very dependent on each other.

If I have any problems it has to do with my loved ones on Earth. I worry about Roger. For a while he wasn't doing anything but recently he's running around. I think he's chasing women. I talked it over with Bea at the Chocolaholic Lounge in the Atrium. I told her Roger just wasn't the type to be on his own for long.

Bea said, "You almost sound like you want to

get him married again."

I told her if the woman was a nice person I probably would be relieved.

"What kind of wife would you choose for Roger?"

"Let's see. She has to be reasonably attractive but not as attractive as me. She can't interrupt Roger when he's reading the *New York Times.* And she has to tell Roger three times to take out the garbage."

"There doesn't seem to be anything difficult about that. What else?"

"She has to be a blonde. Roger always had a thing about Grace Kelly. He never missed any of her movies. His favorite was *High Society.* I once asked him if he had to do it all over again would he have married a blonde *shiksa* and he said, 'That's none of your business.' "

"How can you be a matchmaker if you're in Heaven?" Bea asked.

I took another bite of the double-tiered mousse and suddenly had a brainstorm. "I know! We'll form a committee. We have lots of friends up here who have friends down there who would make good wives. We'll find them and Roger will pursue them."

"This is a dangerous business. Are you sure you want to get that involved in Roger's affairs?"

I ignored the last word.

"I have no choice. I suspect he's in heat and he's going to wind up with someone. I'd rather she be my choice than his."

Roger's Story

People keep asking me why I don't re-marry. The answer is Stella is the only person I've wanted in my life. She was perfect for me.

Before we were married her name was Fisher. She had been an only child and was raised in Forest Hills. Her father was a CPA with his own firm, Arthur Fisher Associates, and both parents doted on her. She went to Forest Hills High School and then to Swarthmore while her father and mother looked for a husband for her. When one didn't come up, she got a job in the home furnishings department at Macy's.

That's where I met her. I was selling fabric while working my way through NYU on a scholarship. Stella said she was attracted to me by the way I wore my tie. It was thrown over my shoulder as if I couldn't care less about anything. I told Stella I wanted to be a scientist and make the world safe for mice and rats and baboons. I said if I could get the Macy's fabric account, I would have enough money to join a fraternity and go to Cape Cod on weekends. Then I asked her out to dinner.

She said yes and we talked late into the night at a club in Manhattan and I decided this lady is worth paying attention to.

We went roller-skating, to the movies and dinner, and I behaved like a perfect gentleman.

At Coney Island, on our fourth date, I tried to touch her bosom and she said angrily, "They're mine."

I told her, "But someday they'll be mine."

She called me a pig. I wasn't insulted. Instead I said: "Someday, Stella, you'll be walking down Madison Avenue past all the posers and wiseguys and it's going to occur to you that you haven't been taking me seriously enough, that I'm everything you want: good-looking, ambitious, caring and romantic. And at that moment it will dawn on you that you're in love with me and if you don't act fast, I could move on."

She told me I was the most conceited man she had ever met. But I was too confident to let it bother me.

On the next date she let me touch her bosoms. I told her they were nicer than Sophia Loren's and she said, "How do you know?"

I said, "We went to high school together."

After that, Sophia Loren was always referred to as "the other woman."

The big moment came when Stella brought me home to meet her parents. They weren't as impressed that I was studying to be a scientist. Her father said, "Unless you have a deal with a pharmaceutical company and deliver what they want, you won't make a buck." Her mother held back on her feelings, waiting to see where my mother lived.

Stella was mortified but I was amused. I told her, "I didn't expect anything more. Forest Hills is full of parents who don't want their daughters to marry scientists. I guess it's the photos of Albert Einstein. He never looked like he could make a buck."

I was beginning to like Stella more and more. As she loosened up she got funnier and more outspoken.

In a month it was her turn to visit my mother in Montclair, New Jersey. Mimi worked full-time as a nurse in a geriatric hospital.

Since I was an only child, Mimi, who worked so hard to raise me, wasn't too pleased that I wanted to leave her for another woman. At our first meal she told Stella what vegetables I wouldn't eat, the pillows I was allergic to, and how smart I was in school. What she was really telling her is that I was the Hope Diamond and there weren't any women who were worthy of me, including her.

On the way back to Manhattan, Stella said, "I don't think she likes me."

"She isn't going to like anybody I bring over. Look at it from her standpoint. She breaks her back and her heart to raise her child and then has to deliver him to another woman who has no idea what it took to make that person what he is."

"Am I going to have to go through that if we have children?"

"It's a possibility," I said. "You know, I'm not doing cartwheels over your parents either."

As we drove through the Lincoln Tunnel she

24

said, "Maybe we should forget it." And she cried all the way under the Hudson River, through to Manhattan and Queens.

A few weeks later I showed up at Macy's with a bouquet of flowers. I also had a ring from Tiffany's tied to a rose. It wasn't one that Elizabeth Taylor would wear but it was what I could afford. When Stella showed it to her mother and father, they were certain I could not support her for the rest of my life.

But she accepted the ring and they had no choice but to announce our engagement and start planning for the wedding.

Her parents' choice for the celebration was the Plaza Hotel. The rationale for the Plaza was that Stella was the only daughter and they wanted to show their friends how high her father would go to finance the nuptials. For a Forest Hills daughter, the Plaza was the only place for a wedding.

Her maid of honor was Shirley Rivlin from Macy's Accessories and the attendants were all cousins from Queens. My best man was Twoey. He showed up with a six-foot-tall Radio City Music Hall Rockette. By this time Twoey was doing well, having developed a half dozen town houses in Hoboken, and he was able to afford tall chorus girls. The Rockette caused quite a stir, particularly among the male guests. Mimi, who was always suspicious of Twoey, said to me later, "How dare he bring a *shiksa* to the wedding?"

I said, "Twoey's Catholic." And all Mimi said

was, "I wonder what his priest would think."

Twoey was fascinated with the ritual where I broke a wine glass with the heel of my shoe. He asked me how much the hotel charged for the glass. I said, "It's thrown in with the corkage charge."

Stella had mixed feelings about Twoey. She wanted to like him because he was my best friend. At the same time, she didn't trust him. He was a part of my youth, and no wife wants to know what her spouse was doing before their marriage.

Stella later told me that at the reception Twoey had turned to her and said, "I'm going to miss him."

Stella said, "He hasn't died."

"This is about as close as someone can get."

Stella also told me she thought Twoey was sticking his finger in her eye by bringing Miss America to the wedding when she was half a foot taller than Stella and had a neckline that plunged a foot deeper.

Two hundred and fifty people were invited to the wedding and two hundred accepted. Stella's mother seemed upset about the people who did not come and told me everyone would have come if it had been a June wedding like she'd wanted when so many people would not have gone to the country yet.

The Fishers and my mother sat at the head table. The main thing her mother and father discussed was who didn't come to the wedding.

"The Schwartzes didn't come," her mother said, "and we went to their daughter's wedding during a snowstorm." Her father said, "Erickson didn't come and I've thrown more law business his way than I have to anyone." Then her mother said, "The Gufastons said they wouldn't be here because they were going to Paris. But they knew about the wedding three months in advance."

I whispered to Stella, "Do you think the people who came are going to get any credit at all?"

She said, "Not much, even if we validate their parking tickets."

Next Mimi said to Stella's father, "How much did this circus cost you?"

By way of answer her father said, "Stella will only get married once."

Mimi raised her eyebrows and said, "I'll bet the flowers could have paid for Roger's four years in college."

Whenever we agonized over how to pay for something, Mimi would say, "Too bad you don't have the money your father gave to the Plaza." This was the start of a very difficult relationship for Stella's parents and also for Stella.

We danced, people made toasts, we cut the cake and Stella threw the bouquet — Mimi caught it. All the men tried to dance with Twoey's girl.

Twoey and I stood at the bar.

"I guess this is goodbye," he said.

"I'm not going to war."

"That's what you think. It's different once you get married. The male bonding just isn't there. Remember how we used to go to the Playboy Club and try to pick up Bunnies?"

"I never did too well, first because they weren't supposed to date us, and second, they were more attracted to you."

"You still had fun. Remember the time we met the two secretaries from Merrill Lynch and took them on the ferry and they got off at Staten Island with the two dock workers instead of us?"

"Stop," I pleaded. "You're making me cry."

"Remember the time we went to Tijuana and got thrown in jail for chasing chickens down Main Street?"

I turned to him and said, "Twoey, will all the fun be gone?"

"There will be fun but it will be a different kind of fun. Barbecues in the backyard, trips to Jones Beach, maybe if you get lucky a week in Key Biscayne. But our kind of fun? No more, laddie."

I had a cognac and then Stella and I went upstairs to the bridal suite, which Mimi told us cost only $500 a night if you have the wedding at the hotel.

Stella and I had done some heavy petting while dating but hadn't consummated our relationship. She told me on our honeymoon she was scared silly. Not of the act, but that she would be no good at it.

We sat on the bed talking about how many

28

babies we wanted, and what we would do with the Nobel Prize money I would win, and when Stella would find time for her thank-you notes for the wedding. We laughed more than you are supposed to on your wedding night. When we finally made love early the next morning, it was the beginning of some very satisfactory moments in bed.

Stella's Story

While Roger was on Earth doing whatever he was doing, Bea and I decided we better run my wife-search idea by Moses.

We found Moses putting divots back into the golf course. When I explained what we planned to do, he didn't like any part of it. He said that people in Heaven should not get involved in the doings of those on Earth. "Since you are living the perfect life you should no longer feel their pain. I would advise you to stay out of Roger's business."

Bea said as we left, "Well, that's clear."

I said, "Moses knows the Ten Commandments, but he doesn't know anything about Roger."

I've always wanted to see Roger succeed, and now that I'm gone I'm worried I can't help him. He needs a woman to help him achieve success.

In my life on Earth tremendous emphasis was put on how you were doing compared to someone else. It started early for me when you were judged on what your father did for a living. In Forest Hills most of the fathers were involved in the cloak and suit business. If this were the case, you were judged by the high price of the clothes your father made. High-end frock fathers were considered better than those kids whose fathers supplied bras and panties to J. C. Penney's. To avoid all the nonsense, my father started his own business as an accountant.

Since I was an only child my parents doted on me and made sure I had everything I needed in order to avoid any psychological problems later on.

One time in school Red Jacobs called me a Jewish princess. I didn't know what that meant but assumed it was an insult. I ran home crying and told my mother. She said, "Well, you are Jewish, and you are our princess, so there's nothing wrong with the name." But it didn't take me long to find out from Nancy Gordon, the smartest girl in school, that I had been insulted and a Jewish princess was a spoiled snob. I vowed after that not to be a Jewish princess. The best way was to join the high school track team. No one accused the fastest miler in school of being a Jewish princess.

We also had a club in high school called the Happy Girls. We met every afternoon in someone's basement or apartment, and the main subject of conversation was boys.

The game we invented was that each girl had to select a boy she had a crush on and tell us of a fictitious affair she had had with him. My choice was Roy Albertson. He was on the tennis team and I told everyone I loved him because he always wore whites.

"So what happened?" Audrey Minderman asked.

"Well, one afternoon after he won his match I got in his car, and he climbed in and just started kissing me."

"Go on."

"He put his hand on my knee and with the other hand he lifted up my shirt and unbuttoned my bra."

"Oh my God," said Jeannie Aiyer. "Did you stop him?"

"What could I do? I couldn't talk. Then he put his hand on my breast. I swooned. Then he kissed me on the stomach. That was it, but I'll never forget it."

The Happy Girls all giggled and said, "Your story is the best."

The end of that story is that Roy Albertson went on to play tennis for Princeton, joined the pro ranks for a couple of years, then finally got a job in a bank where he embezzled $200,000 and was sent to prison for five years.

Roger's Story

Stella and I discuss everything. I talk to her from my bedroom with the window open to the sky so she'll have better reception.

As I said, Stella's reason for being in Heaven is lung cancer. One day she was a happy house-wife, the next she was being examined by Dr. Bill Cahan at Sloan-Kettering. The first thing the doctor wanted to know was if she smoked. She said, "I'll give it up this week."

But it was too late. Stella was an intelligent person, but when it came to cigarettes she wasn't very smart.

Once they arrived at the cancer diagnosis, life for her wasn't much fun. Stella had been a very gregarious person until she got sick. Then she became angry and lashed out at everyone. She was particularly tough on the nurses, which was a surprise because Stella had always been nice to everyone. During her worst moments she kept firing everyone in the house, including her doctor.

I was constantly smoothing people's feelings. Stella wasn't like this all the time. She tried to put on a good front for her visitors but she was tougher on those close to her.

After she passed away Stella kept asking questions about what happened immediately after-wards.

"Tell me the truth, Roger. Was it a good funeral?"

"Are you kidding? It was the best. You know how at funerals, people keep looking at their watches? Well, nobody looked at theirs. It was as if they wanted to stay with you as long as they could."

"Mrs. Gittleson said Rabbi Sparkman went on too long."

"Don't listen to her. She never says anything nice about anything, including your funeral. Besides, maybe she's bitter because she isn't down here to make snide remarks."

"What did Rabbi Sparkman say?"

"He said you were a wonderful wife and mother and the angels were lucky to have you. You could tell he put a lot of work into your eulogy. I told him you would have appreciated everything he said. I gave him a big tip, then he hugged me. You know, you don't usually get hugs from Sparkman."

"Were people crying?"

"Of course they were crying. Your loss was felt by everyone. Connie Friedman told me you touched everybody in the community."

"Was the temple full?"

"Yes. I didn't expect to see such a crowd. Many were from out of town, not counting your relatives from Toledo. Even the National Headquarters of the Hadassah sent a representative. The lady told me this is very rare and only happens if a person had given more than $100,000,

33

which of course we never did. It was a joy to behold. Stella, a nice funeral was always important to you, wasn't it?"

"It was in this respect. You're on Earth for such a short time you're afraid that nobody will know you were there. So a funeral is the last chance for you to say, 'Goodbye, everybody. I was here and I'm glad I meant something to somebody.' Now that I know people were crying, maybe they were sorry I was gone."

"Everyone's sorry you're gone, Stella. Whenever I walk through the neighborhood people stop me and say, 'I miss Stella.' I hope they remember me the same way they remember you."

"One finds no joy in living if no one knows we're alive."

"That's why funerals are for the living, not for the dead."

"What was the reception like?"

"It was lovely. We held it at our house and all your friends brought dishes and looked to see who brought what. Edith Jaffe said, 'Stella always loved my baked bean casserole.' Alice Gordon said, 'I once gave Stella my recipe for gazpacho and she always gave me credit.' Doris Kahme said, 'Next to life, Stella loved chocolate mousse.' "

"How many people were at the house?"

"At least sixty, maybe seventy. They kept showing up and hugging me. They wouldn't look at me, though. I think they were afraid that whatever you had would be passed on to them."

"What about the kids?"

"They hated the whole thing. They said it was awful because they didn't know half the people and they all said such dumb things. Mrs. Wimple said to them, 'Let this be a lesson to you. God is still in charge.'

"Kaplan, the insurance man, came up to Timmy and said, 'I told your father Stella was underinsured, and he wouldn't listen to me. I wanted your mother to carry at least $240,000 straight life. Instead Roger only went for $150,000.' Stella, we have some pain-in-the-ass friends."

"Who didn't show?"

"The Abramovitzes. Zelda sent a note saying they had to be in Florida for a cerebral palsy meeting, which I think is bullshit."

"It doesn't surprise me they didn't come. Once Zelda told me she hated funerals and wouldn't go to one even if it were for a close relative."

"Lauren Decatur brought a box of peanut brittle and said it was your favorite candy. I had to eat it even though I'd already eaten Fern's white bean casserole.

"I swear, Stella, some of the women at the reception were looking me over to see who they could fix me up with."

Stella didn't respond, so I moved on.

"Anyway, people stayed on late. They told stories about you. In the beginning they were serious, but then they got funny. They all kept saying you were a very funny person."

I then asked Stella a question I was terribly curious about.

"What did it feel like to die?"

"I don't remember what it was like. I remember there were strong arms that seemed to lift me to an escalator. You know, I didn't weigh too much. But I didn't have any sense of where I was going or when I would get there. I was just aware of the arms. The next thing I knew I was up here and breathing a sigh of relief that it was nicer than I had imagined it could be."

"Does everyone use a wish to talk to their loved ones on Earth like we do?"

"I don't know. You're not supposed to have secrets up here but we all do. I know one woman whose husband on Earth goes to the racetrack every day. Some days he asks her for nice weather and other days when he is betting a horse that runs well in the mud he asks her for rain."

Then Stella asked me a question. "Roger, have you ever thought about dying?"

"I didn't until you passed away. Now I think about it a lot. I hope when it happens I can join you wherever you are and we can keep going the way we were."

Stella said, "It's not guaranteed. The people who assign places in Heaven are located somewhere in Colorado. No one can be certain where they're going."

"I guess now would be the best time to put in my request."

"One other thing. If you got married again, it could cause complications."

Stella's Story

I know you're wondering what we do with our leisure time in Heaven. Most of it is sitting by the pool and exchanging stories. There are so many stories we can sit here forever. It seems nothing is simple.

Bridey Beamon told us a weird one yesterday. Several years ago she was sitting with her second husband, Fritz, who wasn't much, when her son Cornell, who was twenty-nine years old, came into the room. He confessed to his mother that when he was ten years old his older brother George forced him to commit oral sex on him. Bridey was horrified but all Fritz said was, "That still doesn't give you a right to speak to your mother that way."

I think a lot about the people I left behind. Some were friends, some were conveniences. I once read where the great writer William Styron said he divided the human race into three classes: the well-poisoners, the life-enhancers and the lawn mowers. The well-poisoners need no explanation; the life-enhancers were the smallest group, making things better for all of us. The largest group were the lawn mowers. They didn't look to the right or the left and they didn't know what was going on.

Shortly after my last discussion with Roger there was trouble in Heaven — where you're not supposed to have any trouble. Bea, who as I said had had a very bitter divorce from her husband, Michael, had a traumatic experience. The woman who stole Michael away from Bea slipped in the bathtub onto her head and arrived in Heaven.

"I'll kill her," Bea said.

"You can't kill her. She's already dead."

"I'll put something in her food to make her sick."

"You can't get sick here. Besides, if you're caught trying to cause trouble in Heaven, they'll throw you into the inferno."

"Then what do I do? She's up here and she's going to spoil every moment that I'm in paradise."

"I think you should speak to Moses. I'm sure he has an answer."

We found Moses folding towels. St. Peter could have folded them for him, but Moses said folding towels was very therapeutic and made him feel so much better.

Bea explained her problem to him. He rubbed his whiskers as he does whenever he's thinking. "Broken marriages always give me the most problems. I wish people would obey their vows as prescribed in the Bible."

Bea yelled, "She's a bitch! Once she got her hands on Michael he didn't have a chance. She broke up my home and she doesn't belong in Heaven."

Moses tried to calm her down. "I don't know all the facts. If we had to ban everyone who was divorced, we would only be half-full up here. At the same time we can't afford having people in Heaven who don't like each other. God doesn't like trouble in paradise."

I said, "Then what do you suggest?"

Moses said, "We'll send her to the Four Seasons down the road. It's as nice as the Ritz-Carlton and should solve the problem."

Bea was mollified. As we went to the exercise room she said to me, "No wonder they call him Moses."

Roger's Story

Last night Stella said she wants me to get married again because she doesn't believe I can manage my life alone. I told her I didn't want to get married again. I wasn't completely happy, but I didn't believe my life could be improved by taking on another person. Besides, I wasn't ready to start choosing wallpaper. She became upset.

"It's not safe for you to be out there alone, Roger. Women are waiting to snare men like you. I'm trying to save you. Give me a thirty-day option on finding a wife for you."

I said, "No way," and she hung up on me.

To add to my woes Twoey showed up at the front door the other day with a pair of blonde stewardesses from Scandinavian Airlines. I took him aside and said I was tired and didn't want to go out and my stewardess period was over.

"If you don't go out, we'll come in," Twoey said and the three of them came into the living room. One of the women said to me, "Can we watch wrestling on TV?"

I shrugged and they turned the TV on. We were all sitting around drinking beer when Sarah and Mimi walked in. I introduced everyone but Sarah was about to burst.

"How could you do this to Mom?" she asked in front of everyone.

"What did I do?"

"I don't know but I'm sure it was disgusting."

Mimi looked over the women and said, "I know all about SAS stewardesses. All they're looking for is a good time between LaGuardia and Copenhagen."

Sarah said to the two women, "If my mother were here she would die."

The worst part of being a bachelor is whatever you're doing everyone thinks you're doing worse.

Twoey said, "Ladies, it's time to go," leaving me to deal with Sarah and Mimi. I had done nothing wrong, yet I was indicted and convicted.

When we were alone Mimi said, "You're having another midlife crisis. I've been expecting it any day."

"What's wrong with my having people over to my own house?"

"There is nothing wrong with it if you're not being randy."

Sarah said, "I never thought I'd find my father in the living room with two blondes," then Mimi said, "I never want to see foreign women in my house again."

"It's not your house," I said to her. "And what have you got against foreign women, anyway?"

Sarah said, "You're my father. Don't you have any respect for me at all?"

"So I want a life!" I shouted. "Why is everyone telling me what to do?"

"All we're doing is what Stella would want us to do," Mimi said.

I gave up. The next time I spoke to Twoey I told him if he was coming over, to please leave his girlfriends at home.

Where Twoey was helping was matters of finance. I figured he knew everything when he bought an Armani suit for $1,500. This impressed the hell out of me because I'd never paid more than $15 for an Arrow shirt, two for $25 if I wanted them to last a few years.

What made me dependent on Twoey was six months after Stella's death I received the $150,000 life-insurance policy check that Sam Kaplan had sold me after I beat him at tennis one summer on Long Island.

Twoey said, "Give it to me. I'll make you an associate partner in my next deal." It sounded like a good proposition and Twoey guaranteed me a much better rate of return than I could get at the Chase Manhattan Bank. I signed over the check.

I thought it would be a secret. But Stella told me Prudin the angel said Mrs. Gittleson heard from Sam's wife, Eleanor, that I had come into a large sum of money. I told Stella when she confronted me that it was true and I had bought U.S. Treasury Bonds for the children. Had she known I'd given it to Twoey to invest, she would have had a fit or whatever they have up there.

Seven months later, Twoey came to the lab and told me he had filed for bankruptcy. He found out that the land he'd purchased for his houses had once been used as a dump for toxic oil waste. The environmental inspectors said if anyone struck a match, this part of New Jersey would blow up. To add to his problems, the savings and loan where he'd borrowed his money had gone bankrupt and the government auditors who took it over said Twoey owed them a million dollars. He'd thought he'd made a smart move when he'd bought the land at a bargain price.

At this point I started thinking about jumping off the Empire State Building. Twoey discussed his trouble as if he were describing a New York Yankee game. He played catch with a bottle of L-lysine and said this kind of thing happened to builders all the time.

I was in shock. Twoey said, "What say we go

to a bar and pick up a couple of chicks?"

"How can you talk about women when I just lost all my savings?"

"Those are the breaks," Twoey said.

I sank into a swivel chair. "My biggest fear is that somehow Stella will find out about it."

Twoey looked at me like I was the one with the really big problem.

"Roger, it's only money. Would you stop spinning in that chair already?"

I stopped. I was really angry. "Why didn't you find out it was polluted before you went in?"

"It didn't smell polluted."

"What did it smell like?"

"You know." He was grinning. "New Jersey."

I couldn't help but smile but I was still ticked off.

"Roger, once I get some more money I'll double your investment. I have a project I'm looking at in Bronxville. It's perfect for a highrise. Your money isn't lost, it's just in escrow. Trust me."

I threatened to break off my relationship with Twoey. He said, "You couldn't do that even if you wanted to. We're bonded by our history — with women."

The real difference between Stella and him was that while Stella had someone matronly in mind, Twoey kept introducing me to divorcees who liked to go around the world on cruises, play tennis in England and spend time at the Golden

43

Door to have themselves made over. "These women are expensive," I complained to Twoey.

He laughed. "Most of them have money of their own. Besides, they don't know it but they all need a good boff."

He told me I didn't realize how much I was worth to women of a certain age.

One of the more bizarre moments of Twoey's matchmaking efforts was a date with a starlet who was in an off-Broadway play. After the show we went for supper at Elaine's. She was interested in my work in herpes for about two minutes and then wanted to discuss the theater, which I knew nothing about. Finally she invited me up to her apartment. When we arrived there were five locks on the door. She opened each one and then when we got inside she said, "Go into the bedroom."

I did.

"Now go into the living room."

I checked the living room.

"The kitchen."

I looked over the kitchen.

Then she said, "Good night."

As I walked to the door I turned to her and said, "Do you always ask guys to come up and check out your rooms before you go to bed?"

"Of course. You never know who might be hiding here."

As she held the door open for me I asked her, "Can I ask you a question?"

She spread her hands out.

"Why do you live in New York?"

44

She said, "I wouldn't live anyplace else."

Every once in a while I realize how much Stella kept me from getting into the kind of trouble Twoey was always getting himself into. She provided me with support, advice and nourishment. Now I have no center. The decisions she made were written in stone. Now I don't know whether to go to the movies or the beach, do the laundry or have it done, or just leave it all for the next week.

I guess Stella's reason to want me to get married again is so I'll know what to do.

Stella's Story

Sometimes I miss my old friends on Earth, not just Roger. The best visit I had during my illness was from the Happy Girls. Three of them showed up: Audrey Minderman, Mary Beach and Cathy Clark. They were all dressed up in their finest and each one brought me a box of Godiva chocolates. Audrey said, "We didn't know whether to dress up or dress down for you today. We finally decided you'd rather see us looking decent."

It hurt to laugh but I did.

"Genie Altman said to tell you she was sorry she couldn't make it but her gym trainer wouldn't change her time."

Mary said, "You're not serious about leaving the club?"

I said, "It's possible."

"The Happy Girls can't live without you," Cathy said.

"Consider the alternative."

We then chatted about our men. Several of the Happy Girls were into their second marriages, two were into their third. The children of the members were either successful or were still trying to "find their way" in their thirties.

The nurse had told them to stay only for an hour. But at my insistence they remained for three. They made me feel so much better.

Each of them kissed me before they left. They all promised to see me again. But we knew it would be our last visit.

In the case of cancer, people ask, "Where is it?" as if that changes things. I used to get so angry answering that one that I wanted to dump dishwater on their heads. Then I realized that people asked this because they were concerned for themselves. If you say "lung," they touch their chests to check to see if there are any pains there; with "stomach," they check their stomachs. People don't ask where there is trouble when it comes to heart attacks. They all know where the heart is.

I guess people are always dealing with avoiding illness and when an acquaintance is very, very sick, they want the details just in case they can prevent it from happening to them.

One of the worst things about knowing you are going to die involves the decisions to be made.

Who do you tell and what do you tell them? The very toughest part of dying is that weeks and months before we go the phone rings all the time. Some people have nothing to say, but they take up a lot of time. They tell you about their uncle Fred and their father and a distant relative named Laura. Then there are those who bring food to the door because with food you have to let them in.

All sorts of strange things happen when you're dying. Although Sarah and I were at war most of her life, when the end was near Sarah took over and allied herself with me. Sarah told everyone what I wanted and she said I wanted it pronto. I recall one time when I asked to go downstairs and Sarah announced she would take me. I was all bones and Roger said "no" and Timmy said *"no!"* and the nurse said "NO!" We had a battle, Sarah and I on one side and the rest of the family on the other. They wouldn't carry me downstairs and Sarah yelled, "She's my mother!" and she carried me all by herself.

That night at dinner she told everyone a person should be able to do what she wants before she dies.

Roger's Story

Stella wouldn't let up on finding a mate for me.

"You know who would make a good wife for

you?" she said last night. "Molly Lowenstein. She lost her Philip six months ago and Mrs. Gittleson says she's on the prowl."

"Stella, do we have to go through this?"

"Why not? You obviously can't handle money on your own. And you're still a catch. Men like you don't come along very often. Most of them get grouchier as they get older. But you have a good disposition and never complain. I was the one who always complained. Many women like a man who doesn't do anything at home except take out the garbage. You're not a take-charge kind of guy. Molly Lowenstein would be lucky to get you."

"I'm going out to get a beer."

Stella said, "Roger, are you sure you're getting enough to eat?"

I said, "I go out to restaurants a lot. When they have rice pudding on the menu, I order it. You know how much I love rice pudding, particularly if it has raisins in it, and especially if you made it."

What I didn't tell Stella was that I ate dinner quite often with Twoey. She never approved of him while she was alive, and I'm certain she didn't approve of him now.

Twoey has been married three times so far. After we parted from high school he went into business, first working for a contractor and then by himself. Before I met Stella, Twoey always knew a stewardess who knew a divorcée who knew someone who played around. I was best

48

man at his first, second and third marriages. Somehow he managed to remain in the Catholic Church, which shows you what kind of operator Twoey is.

After we got married I had to see Twoey on the sly since Stella made such a fuss when he showed up at the house. She considered Twoey a nuclear threat.

Something Stella didn't know is that during our marriage I'd invested in Twoey's construction projects once before and they'd paid off handsomely. If you look from Manhattan across to Hoboken you'll see a dozen town houses of which I own a small piece. The investment came from money I had squirreled away from bonuses and writing about herpes. It wasn't much but Twoey turned it into a nest egg. It provided the Folger family with money we wouldn't have had.

Twoey was not disturbed that Stella didn't approve of him. "Women are always nervous around successful men," he said.

After Stella died Twoey came back in the picture as running buddy and best friend. He told me, "You're not safe out there alone. You need a woman. A *consigliere*." He had just seen *The Godfather* for the tenth time that weekend.

Though I'm still having to deal with an awful lot of emotional stuff over Stella dying, I was fortunate that I did have a last conversation with Stella before she passed away. I was sitting in bedroom late at night. We had just watched

49

sablanca on the television. Stella said, "I feel like Ingrid Bergman when she said goodbye to Humphrey Bogart."

I laughed and said, "I never thought of myself as Humphrey Bogart. I'm more the Jimmy Stewart type."

"I think it's time for me to go, Roger."

"No way. I need you."

"Be sure and pay Edna, the cleaning woman, once a week."

"Stella. Please don't go."

"You should paint the living room. I noticed there were brown spots on the ceiling."

"Of course."

"Sarah has to keep the kitchen clean now that I'll no longer be there. And be sure to take the car in for a tune-up every three months. I was the only one in the family who did it faithfully. Also make certain Timmy and Sarah go to the dentist every six months, and don't forget to get a haircut."

Tears were pouring down my cheeks. Stella seemed quite content. I held her hand. It was cold like the time we went to New Hampshire in October.

When Stella died, Timmy was the only one there. He told me that he felt God had rewarded him for spending so much time with her and after not being able to be there when his best friend died in Vietnam.

I arrived minutes later. I called the doctor and he called the police. What people don't know is

that in the event of a death, the homicide squad has to be notified immediately to make sure that there has been no foul play. They were the ones who released Stella to the funeral home. But they had to get their supervisor's permission and he was out to dinner. So we sat around in the living room, discussing the Yusef Hawkins case. It was weird that we were discussing Bensonhurst as if nothing else had happened.

The police finally told their boss that there was no foul play and the Smith Brothers Funeral Home took Stella away.

Everyone was in shock although it shouldn't have come as a surprise. Once Stella was taken to the Smith Brothers Funeral Home they sold me their most expensive coffin and said, "Stella may not know what you paid but relatives and friends will." Timmy told the director to dress Stella in her favorite nightgown.

Death is something no one is prepared to deal with. And since we don't want to give it thought, we don't have experience with it.

The night before her funeral people came to bestow their regrets. The kids and I manned the door of the home and received those who wanted to come by and those who were making an obligatory visit. Everyone meant well but we had to listen to a lot of crap because people have nothing to say at this moment but they have to say something.

The relatives came in from out of town and we had to take care of them, provide transportation and find housing for those who didn't have any hotels. Some people I had never seen in my life showed up. At the front door one man said, "I saw it in the newspaper," so we let him in too. So the strange thing about the initial grieving period was you have to satisfy so many strangers. Timmy told me, "We should have had the funeral in Las Vegas."

The ride to the cemetery was more meaningful because the kids and I were in the limousine and we could share each other's grief without all the others. Stella was in the hearse in front of us, once again leading the family on the journey.

By then Timmy and Sarah and I knew the good guys from the bad guys. Take Myra Zale. Even after Stella passed away, Myra tried to get into the house to check out everything and possibly help herself to something she thought would not be missed. I am not saying she took anything, but I wouldn't put it past her.

The ceremony at the cemetery was even more beautiful than the one in the synagogue. For one thing it had rained all day but stopped before the prayers at the grave. People gathered around and Sarah, Timmy and I each placed a stone on the coffin. The whole thing looked like a Fellini movie. Those who came to the cemetery to say goodbye got their money's worth.

Stella told me, "I'm glad it rained. If it had been a nice day, my parting would not have had any meaning."

I assured her it had plenty of meaning.

Feeling guilty about the insurance money, I called Stella last night just to chat.

"I'm a good man and I try to be nice, but since I've become a widower people treat me differently. For some women I'm just a warm body, a trophy to be introduced to everyone. Others are attracted to me because I listen to their stories and I worry about them. Some have money problems. Mary Broadloom didn't make her mortgage. So I helped her out. Her boyfriend thought she was sleeping with me and said he was going to kill me. Fortunately I know Arnie Zeigler, a sergeant in the NYPD who helped us with Sarah when she was found smoking pot in Washington Square Park. He went to see the boyfriend and told him he would run him over in a police car if he so much as contacted me again. It was a nice thing for Zeigler to do but it was a situation I never thought I'd get into in a million years."

Stella said, "I knew you'd have problems as soon as I was gone. This is what I say: Stop helping so many people."

"Do you know I have three health-insurance policies out at this moment for people who couldn't otherwise get them? I think this is a good idea because people never tell you that they don't have health insurance, yet it's the most important insurance anyone can have."

"How did you get into health insurance?"

"Remember Gerry, the taxi driver who helped us when our car was set on fire? One day he told me his son had asthma and he couldn't fill the prescription because it was fifty-six dollars. I asked him if he had health insurance and he told me he couldn't afford it, so I bought a Blue Cross policy for him."

"Roger, that's a nice thing but people can take advantage of you. It doesn't matter as much with men but it does with women. I hate to say this but when it comes to women you're chopped liver. They sense it just like the UJA knows how much money you can afford to give. Forget your personalized philanthropy and give a small donation to the American Red Cross."

"But when I give to individuals I can hear them say thank you. The American Red Cross or the Anti-Defamation League never says thank you. They just say could I give more. Why are you so interested in all this, anyway?"

"Because it's my insurance money that you're spending. Are you going to invest it in a mutual fund?"

I thought to myself, she doesn't know.

I said, "I was thinking of something like that."

That seemed good enough and Stella got off the phone to watch *Fantasia* with Bea.

Stella's Story

Yesterday Prudin came to me and said, "Did you hear your husband lost all your insurance money

54

in a bad oil investment?"

"What are you talking about?"

"Kitzler the banker killed himself yesterday and he just told me."

"Who's he?"

"He was the president of the Skulnik Savings and Loan, where your husband's partner Twoey borrowed two million dollars. When they came to audit Kitzler's books they found out he was stealing from everyone's accounts. That's when Kitzler decided to check out from the window of the thirtieth floor."

Of course I was furious. I immediately called Roger and said, "Someone told me you lost all my insurance money in a housing scheme."

Roger sounded calm. "Relax, Stella. It's a temporary setback. We should have everything back in a month plus twenty percent more."

"That means the kids get nothing."

"Twoey says when our ship comes in they'll never have to work a day in their lives."

I was so angry.

"How dumb can you get?"

"Like Twoey said, life's a gamble and the only ones who get swamped are those who don't know when to shoot craps."

I hung up on him.

Mimi heard about the insurance money disaster the same time I did. Like everything Roger did, it soon became public knowledge. Mimi told Roger she was surprised I was worth $150,000. She felt it was Roger's money and he could do anything he wanted with it.

Even up here Mimi gets the best of me.

Mimi must have been put on Earth to torture me. Since Roger was her only child she was devoted to him. But instead of fairy tales she recited horror stories to him about his father. Roger used to wake up in the night because he saw his father in his nightmares. When this happened Mimi would come into the room, hold him and tell him another horror story.

She was tough. At our wedding she told me, "He may be yours in marriage, but he's mine in blood."

I thanked her for the warm greeting.

During our marriage she called every day and Roger held on to the phone for dear life. Sometimes when she visited us she would say to Roger, "You look terrible. That's because she doesn't clean." She was wrong. I was scrubbing all the time.

When Timmy was eighteen and Sarah was sixteen, Mimi was thrown out of her apartment because she wasn't supposed to have a cat. She asked if she and Fluffinutter could live with us for a few weeks until she could find another place to stay.

What could we say? More important, what could I say? The two weeks turned into seven years. She refused to leave even when Fluffy died.

Sarah agreed to share her room with her, which turned out to be the biggest mistake of our parenting. They became fast friends and took turns driving Roger and me crazy.

All Sarah's friends thought Mimi was "groovy." She hung out with them at the 7-Eleven and rode on the backs of their motorcycles. She claimed to be the only senior citizen who had spent all her Social Security money on a leather jacket and a Harley helmet.

Several times I threatened to leave home and get a divorce if Mimi did not move out. I had a lot of good reasons. Once Roger got sick and I cooked matzo ball soup. Mimi said, "It tastes like Windex." That was the last straw.

I packed and went to a Holiday Inn. Timmy found me and talked me into coming back and Mimi and I negotiated a UN treaty with his help. Mimi was never to mention anything about my cooking and I would never mention anything about her deceased cat.

This didn't stop Mimi reminding Roger at dinner of the wonderful meals she had cooked for him. It was a bad night when I served meat loaf or spaghetti.

At this point Sarah was wearing a ring in her nose. She said she was making a statement. When we asked her what that statement would be she said it was for her generation to know and us to find out.

At dinner Mimi couldn't stop staring at Sarah with the gold ring in her nose. "What does that do to your breathing?" she asked her.

"Nothing."

Mimi turned to Roger and said, "You don't think the gold ring in her nose is just showing off?"

Roger always turned into a coward in his mother's presence and he shrugged. Just to get her I said, "It doesn't hurt anybody."

Mimi said, "It hurts me."

This is why I really hated Mimi. She made me side with Sarah when I really thought the gold ring was disgusting.

It was a merry household. Sarah decided the best way to get me was to play up to Mimi. Mimi, who didn't approve of a lot of things Sarah did, decided if it was going to drive me crazy she would take Sarah's side, and Roger took his mother's side because he couldn't stand the heat in the kitchen.

I kept biting my tongue to keep from asking Mimi to get out of my house.

Mimi was constantly getting involved in protest rallies. She was especially big on labor and civil rights. One day she disappeared to join a march, and the Ku Klux Klan burned our car — the whole car.

When I told Bea about this she said she'd had a mother-in-law who behaved the same way. They picked her up for drunken driving and it cost $1,000 and she had to go to driver's reeducation school. Her second husband, a mama's boy, told everyone he was proud of her when she graduated.

As far as Mimi was concerned, her greatest triumph was when she and Sarah went to Washington to protest the Vietnam War. Once I found the two of them in their bedroom on the floor practicing to be arrested and thrown into a police wagon. They told me it was the only way they could stop General Westmoreland from issuing more body counts. Roger was not against civil disobedience. He was just concerned the Klan would burn our new car.

Mimi and Sarah's big moment came when the two went to Washington one hot day in May. They took the train with hundreds of other protesters, and Mimi led everyone in singing "This Land Is Your Land" and "Study War No More." They also shouted obscenities about the Pentagon.

When they got to Washington they marched in front of the White House. Sarah said the FBI was taking pictures of everybody, and Mimi kept shouting that Richard Nixon was a flaming transvestite.

What made Mimi's trip a success is that *The Washington Post* ran a front-page photo of her throwing a rotten egg at Henry Kissinger's limo. She looked like Sandy Koufax in the photo and kept it over her bed.

After that most of the Queens anti-war movement started to congregate at our house, where Mimi served tea and cinnamon toast. They liked that. What they didn't know was that there was a milk truck parked down the street inside of which men in dark suits were monitoring them.

Within a week a platoon of FBI agents came to the door, flashing identification shields.

Mimi shouted, "Take me. Put me in prison, rape me. I will never tell you where I hid my Viet Cong flag."

This would have been amusing but when the FBI ran a check on Mimi, they found that Roger was her son and had a high government clearance from the chemical company that he worked for. The company required everyone to be cleared, even if they weren't involved in defense work. Besides, finding a cure for herpes during the Vietnam War was considered top-secret work because the CIA had reported the Russians were working on the same thing. Boy, was Roger in trouble and was I good and mad.

Prudin the angel is spreading rumors as usual. It was from her that I heard Ronnie Sandler had heard that Roger was seen in an Italian restaurant with a blonde woman choking with jewels. Apparently, Twoey was with him with another young lady. Ronnie had heard it from her sister, who's still down on Earth. She told me Roger was shocked to see Jane and pretended the blonde was a business associate. I told Ronnie it was none of my business, but it made me mad as hell. Not the idea of Roger dating so much as the thought that he was taking out women without telling me.

When I confronted Roger, he said, "Women say I have a very sympathetic ear and really listen to them. What makes them lonely is that it's hard to find someone they can really talk to. My ears seem to be the thing they find the most attractive about me."

Roger's Story

Last week to get back in Stella's good graces, I went out with one of her choices for a date who turned out to be a commando from the 1960s Women's Lib Movement. Rachel Steiglitz was a "feminist theorist" and saw gender abuse everywhere. I took her out twice. The first time she lectured me on equal pay for women athletes, a situation I can't change. The second time we went out she told me the biggest mistake women made was letting men use their bodies for pleasure.

When I told Twoey about this conversation, he said, "It sounds like she needs it badly."

I said, "Stella must be crazy to think I want to get mixed up with somebody who wants to keep lecturing me all the time."

The next time I spoke to Stella I asked her what she had in mind with hooking me up with this woman.

She said, "She wasn't my idea, she was Bea's. She thought you needed a heavyweight fighter for your second wife."

I said, "I want out."

"You gave us a month," Stella said.

I told her I would rather read a book.

Stella seemed as upset about Twoey and me as the time I came home and announced I had been fired. Mimi and Sarah both said they were proud of me. I was more practical and inquired what we were going to do for income. I could find another job but the law forbade me from taking any of my herpes secrets with me.

Timmy suggested I try to find a cure for Vietnam jock itch. I told him that this also required a government clearance. With the usual twinkle in his eye, Timmy suggested that I go to the FBI and turn Mimi and Sarah in as Communist spies.

Stella's Story

Let me finish my story about Roger losing his job. Things were getting desperate at home. After Roger got fired, he received severance pay but he had no luck each day he went out looking for work. It doesn't take long for a person to get discouraged when job hunting. Friends Roger had had for years were even frightened for themselves and they avoided us. When they checked on his status with the employment agencies, they found out he was a tough case.

My heart went out to him when he came home at night. He kept saying, "I never thought this would happen in America. No one knows what it's like to lose your job. You lose your nerve. For years my world was the end of a microscope. Now I'm facing the real world and it's a degrading place to be."

After a few weeks I made a decision. I would go back to work and at least we would have some cash flow. I got my job back at Macy's.

Gloria Auerbach in charge of Home Furnishings was still there, and she got me a position as a lamp buyer. It was a blow to Roger, who thought his role in the family was the breadwinner.

It turned out to be a great experience for me because for the first time in years I was dealing with grown-ups every day. I realized how out of touch you can become as a housewife. The only reality you know is what you hear on the talk shows or what your kids bring home from school.

Timmy got a job delivering Pete's Pizza. He told the family with pride, "You have to be fast on your feet or the customers get the pizza for free. I get there in time and my customers always pay."

As a matter of fact, if someone asked what kind of son I would want, I couldn't wish for a better one than Timmy. He was beautiful and he was wise. He also had a mind of his own. The big event in Timmy's life as far as my parents were concerned was his *bar mitzvah.*

In Forest Hills you celebrate in the basement of the temple or hire a catering hall on Long

Island or go for broke and rent a room at the Hilton or the Pierre.

As Timmy's big day came I opted for the Plaza but my parents heard the Pierre was the place for it and they would chip in. We were shocked when Timmy announced he didn't want a *bar mitzvah*.

I said, "You can't say that. My parents have been waiting all these years to *bar mitzvah* you."

Timmy said, "It has nothing to do with religion. All we're doing is showing off. I'm willing to go to a rabbi and read from the Torah, but no party."

"But, what about all the gifts?" Roger asked.

"I don't want presents. They have nothing to do with God."

I thought my parents would *plotz* when they heard this outrageous idea, but we survived that one, even with the loss of a couple of friends who couldn't get a return on their gifts.

Anyway, back to my story. While I was enjoying work more than I wanted to admit, Roger was going deeper and deeper into a depression. I finally persuaded him to see Dr. Lenz. This was before they had any of these designer antidepressants. Dr. Lenz told Roger, "You're depressed because you don't have a job."

"That's very wise of you, Dr. Lenz. What do you suggest I do?"

"Get a job."

"I wish I had thought of that."

We were in bad shape. Mother and Father offered to pitch in, but Roger and I wanted no help from that quarter.

There was some talk of asking Mimi to pay rent but that idea flew out the window when Mimi said, "Jewish sons don't ask their mothers to pay room and board." My reply to that was "Jewish mothers don't make their sons lose their jobs."

Roger's firing did not make us a dysfunctional family; we were that already. It just made us a family who was worried about money all the time. The frills went fast. The first to go was Roger's new car, which he replaced with a beat-up, used Chevy. The beauty parlor was the next thing. This hurt because the beauty parlor was the center of Forest Hills' social life. We even canceled the Book-of-the-Month Club. The big saving was the $5,000 a year for the country club. Roger said, "It's no fun playing gin rummy when you don't have a job."

Everyone was afraid to come home at night in fear that Roger would lash out. There was no banter anymore. Even Sarah and Mimi were quiet. There was also no joy in eating. We had all lost our appetites. It seems eating has to do with happiness.

It was two months before Roger got a job working in a drug warehouse as a clerk. He was also determined to clear up the security business. Twoey found him a civil liberties lawyer who just charged expenses. The lawyer said Roger's case was interesting because the FBI had nothing on him, absolutely nothing. All they had were pictures of his daughter and mother throwing rotten eggs at Henry Kissinger.

The big question was whether Roger should go public with the story. The fear was the publicity would hurt the family and do nothing to get back Roger's security clearance.

So the lawyer took the middle ground and filed a motion demanding the FBI produce evidence that Roger was a security risk. He threatened to take the case to the newspapers if they didn't respond.

A week later two hefty agents came to the door to speak to Roger. He wasn't home, so I invited them in to speak to me.

The one with the sandpaper face said, "Does your husband go to meetings that you don't know about?"

"How would I know if I don't know about it?" I answered.

"Has he ever discussed the Ho Chi Minh Trail in favorable terms?"

"Not that I know of. He's a Knicks fan and whenever he has a spare moment he talks about basketball."

The agent wearing cowboy boots said, "Did your husband drive your mother-in-law to Washington to the anti-war rallies?"

"No, the girls took the train. They said it made them closer to 'the people.' "

"Do you mind if we take a look at your books in your library?"

"Go ahead. We belong to the Book-of-the-Month Club and subscribe to *World Book Encyclopedia* but our biggest collection has to do with herpes."

Cowboy Boots said, "That isn't funny."

Then I got really mad. "You've destroyed the career of a good man and a great scientist who has no interest in hurting the government, all because you have film of his mother and daughter protesting a lousy war which is sucking this country dry. You're supposed to be finding criminals and mobsters and spies. Instead you waste your time checking out what people are reading. You should be ashamed of yourselves and so should J. Edgar Hoover, who everybody knows is a cross-dresser."

Sandpaper got red in the face and said, "I don't care what you say about us. But you can't talk that way about the Director."

"Why not?"

"Because it will have to go in my report."

The FBI realized that they had no case but it still took a lot of red tape before Roger got his security clearance back. They talked to the neighbors, who were frightened silly. The agents even went to Macy's to find out if I belonged to any anti-war sympathizers in the Gift Wrapping department.

It took six months. When Roger returned to the lab, management greeted him like a long-lost brother in spite of the fact no one fought for Roger when he was defamed. He went back to his herpes research with the hope that some kind of algae might be the cure.

Sarah and Mimi maintained they had done nothing wrong in protesting the war and refused to be blamed for what had happened to Roger, which made me twice as furious with both of them. I banned any more anti-war demonstrators from meeting in my house. "If you want to overthrow the government," I told them, "find a basement in a Chinese restaurant."

Roger's Story

I had big news for Stella. Sarah had become pregnant. This came at an awkward time because she had also told me a few weeks before that she wanted to go to landscape school at Harvard. Sarah said the father was a one-night stand who played in a rock band and was unavailable for a serious relationship.

Stella wanted to know how it happened.

"I wasn't there," I said. When she told me to stop with the sarcasm I said, "I'm sure it was consummated either in a car, or at a Holiday Inn in Atlantic City."

"Well, does she want the child?"

"I think she does. Then again she also wants to live in a hut in Tibet. What am I going to do with a baby in the house? I wish you would talk to her."

"She never listened to me before. She's not going to listen to me now." She paused then said, "I think it's kind of nice she wants the baby."

Stella's Story

The truth is, the thought of Sarah having a baby is giving me waves of nausea.

I have loved Sarah ever since she was a baby and she has loved me, although we had problems communicating after she discovered the Grateful Dead. Sarah was a beautiful baby and Roger and I adored her. So did Mother and Father. From birth Timmy seemed to do his own thing and we ignored him and gave all our attention to Sarah, who couldn't get enough of it.

Our first big mistake was sending her to one of those liberal schools where they permit the students to call their teachers by their first names.

The school had no dress code. There was actually no code for anything so the kids showed up with gold rings in their noses and took smoke breaks with their teachers in the faculty-student lounge.

Sarah was very creative and drew pictures and painted oil paintings of Nixon as a devil sitting on a toilet on the moon, sending bolts of lightning down on the Statue of Liberty. Despite the subject matter, they were good works of art and Roger referred to them as "Sarah's Blue Period."

Our main concern about Sarah was the marijuana we found in her room. She was sixteen years old and we had a deathly fear something terrible would happen to her health or worried about her being caught with the stuff in her rucksack.

One evening Roger and I decided to try some of Sarah's pot to see what it was all about. We didn't know what you had to do to get high.

I said, "I think you're supposed to inhale."

Roger tried to inhale and wound up with a coughing fit. I thought I had inhaled but nothing happened. Neither one of us got anything out of it.

At that moment Sarah caught us and scolded us for smoking her pot. It became part of the family folklore.

I didn't want Sarah to be a member of the Junior League, but at the same time I was hoping she would go to Barnard and meet a nice boy from the Five Towns and sail to Barbados for their honeymoon.

Sarah had other ideas. I blame all of it on the rock bands blasting from her room. Sarah said the music had a voice of its own and took her to places her parents could never go.

The key word in her vocabulary was injustice. There were dozens of forms of injustice and people who hated rock were the most unjust of all. We had to concede that we'd raised a bleeding-heart liberal. Although Sarah didn't have the energy to clean her room she still would fight for the lost tribes of the rain forest. We, her parents, decided to provide the money for the rock concerts because by purchasing the ticket we knew exactly where she was. Row 34 Seat 7. When Sarah went to Woodstock, Roger and I got down on our knees next to the TV set to see if we could find her in the crowd.

Despite all this Sarah did well in school. Still, we were concerned that she would become seriously involved in drugs. We consulted Dr. Lenz, who played gin rummy with Roger at the country club now that Roger had a job again. He said he would talk to her. After his session with her he called Roger and me into his office.

"What do you think?" I asked.

"She's anti-social."

Roger said, "Good work, Fred."

"I asked her if she took drugs and she said no. But she did add that if she did take them she wouldn't tell me."

I said, "You're a miracle man to get that out of her."

He suggested that we keep an eye on her because her obsession with the Grateful Dead could be a cry for help. Then he charged us $175.

Roger and I decided to send Sarah to a fancy prep school where she was safe from all the slings and arrows of her generation. The only problem was that no fancy school would accept her with a gold ring in her nose. She was adamant about not taking it off and so we hit a brick wall.

71

A compromise was reached. If we didn't make Sarah go to boarding school, she would take the ring off. She would be home but we wouldn't have to stare at the ring.

What it added up to was more wars between Sarah and me. It didn't matter what the battles were about. I hated her boyfriends. They would come into the house with no shoes on and head for the refrigerator without even saying hello. They spent their time in Sarah's room listening to all that racket someone decided was music.

Some of the girlfriends were no better. They treated me like the mother of all zombies. I finally forbade Sarah to have any guests in the house. This set her off and she said if her friends could not come into the house, neither would she. It was time for her to run away.

Roger's Story

With Sarah pregnant I was thinking a lot about what it was like to raise her. When Sarah ran away I was in charge of looking for her. Fortunately, she always left enough clues so we could find her. She usually selected a boarding school that a friend was attending. I found Sarah in the student dormitory of the Nottingham School, which her friend Holly was attending. I crashed in at midnight. Sarah was in Holly's room. I begged her to come home, telling her how sorry we were. She wouldn't budge.

Finally Holly said, "For Christ's sake, you're her father. Get her ass out of here."

The kid made sense and I dragged Sarah out of the room and into the car. This was before there was "parenting" and being the head of the family did the job.

Sarah made a few passes at running away again but never got very far.

After Twoey lost my money I told him I never wanted to see him again. He showed up at the house the next weekend with a big smile on his face.

"I've solved all our problems," he said. "There's this rich babe who owns her own shoe company, has a private airplane and houses in Florida and the Dominican Republic. She is also well-built and likes to fool around."

"What has that got to do with me?"

"She's loaded and asked me to fix you two up."

"She doesn't know me."

"She saw you in the Oak Room with me and took a liking to you. She is the kind of woman who always gets what she wants."

"I'm still not interested."

"Wait, there's more. I told her you have a fantastic investment in New Jersey and you might tell her about it. Roger, this is our only chance to get our money back."

"We're going to merge with a shoe company?"

"I'll spring for the '21' Club."

I didn't want to go but when Twoey gets persuasive I always give in.

Mrs. Roundley was all decked out when we met at '21.' She had on everything from Bulgari to David Webb dripping from her neck and Harry Winston on her ears and fingers. I didn't know how old she was because a tremendous amount of work had been done to her face.

We were a merry trio: Mrs. Roundley wanted to talk shoes, Twoey preferred to discuss real estate, and I just sat there wondering when I could go home.

Mrs. Roundley was rubbing my leg under the table. When she finally got up to go to the ladies' room, I said to Twoey, "She's playing with me under the table."

"Great," said Twoey. "That means we're almost out of the woods."

When Mrs. Roundley came back she finally said, "I have my car outside. I'll drop you off."

Twoey said, "I'll walk." Then he pulled me aside and whispered, "She's all yours."

The next morning Twoey called me and asked, "Well? What happened?"

"Nothing happened."

"What do you mean, nothing happened?"

"She has herpes, you dumb bastard."

"How do you know?"

"What do you think I do for a living?"

Now the reports were out among my friends

that I had been seen at '21' with a shoe mogul who owns her own airplane.

Stella must have heard about it from Prudin because in our next conversation she said, "Before we talk about Sarah's pregnancy, tell me, what does Sarah say when you bring a woman into the house?"

"I don't bring women into the house. If I did, Sarah would assume like everyone else that I want to marry the woman."

"Are you thinking about it?"

"I've thought about it but I'm not ready."

"I wouldn't be mad, you know."

"Stella, I haven't met anybody who measures up to you. You spoiled me for another person."

"Stop with the garbage. You'd be a good catch. You're still working, you have a few bucks and you're a good dancer. By the way, you never talk about your work anymore. You only talk about your women and the kids' problems."

"I didn't know you were interested in my work. I thought you were only interested in my women."

"It would break up our conversations a bit."

"The lab work is going well. I'm still looking for the cure. But just when I think I've found a clue, the thing blows up in my face. At least one quarter of the population in America has genital herpes now. If we can find a cure, we're going to save the human race. I have a hotshot Chinese grad student working for me and we're leaping over A all the way to Z. I know we'll figure it out this time."

"I never did understand what you did. Father was frightened silly when he heard you were working on herpes. He was afraid you'd bring it home with you and infect the family."

"I know but he complained about everything I did, so my herpes research was just one more thing. It isn't easy to be around cynics when you're trying to save the world."

"Well, I assumed you knew what you were talking about in spite of the fact that you couldn't change a fuse."

"Fuses are for idiots, herpes is for geniuses. Maybe you should have married an accountant like your father said."

"You're being unfair to my father, Roger, and you're showing no respect for me."

"Stella, how can you lay a guilt trip on someone while you're in Heaven?"

"I'm not laying a guilt trip on you. You worked hard and you were a good provider. I was proud of what you did, even if I never understood it. I always bragged to everyone that you were going to do something important in your research that would save people's lives. Some were impressed but others, I'll admit, said, 'So how come he drives a lousy car?' We weren't rich but we managed to send our children to college and we went to New Hampshire for our vacations and, thanks to money that Father left me, we took that wonderful trip to Paris and Italy.

"I loved Europe. Many of the people up here, particularly the senior citizens, talk about their travels after their spouses passed away. They say that if they hadn't gone to Heaven they would go back to Venice. Last week there was a little bragging going on, which you're not supposed to do up here. Flo Duckbaum said she did both the Atlantic and Pacific cruises with a trip to Antarctica on the same ship as Walter Cronkite."

Stella's Story

I had successfully sidetracked the conversation by getting Roger to talk about his work. I didn't want to frighten him by letting him know the search for a wife was on in earnest after Prudin's story about that rich shoe lady. And Sarah pregnant and Timmy poor — *Oy!*

I drew up a list of prospects from my bridge club and the Brandeis Book Club. They had to be widows and they had to be blonde. The age range was forty-five to sixty. I eliminated women who'd never been married before because they would not know what to do with a man.

I made Bea my sounding board. She said she knew some classy women from Westchester who were getting more desperate for a man every day.

"The problem, Bea, is how I get Roger to meet them."

Bea thought it might be a good idea if we turned it over to Moses.

Moses was at the outdoor snack bar by the

pool, making margaritas. We told him what was bothering us.

"This is not the first time the question has come up," he said. "Most widows want their husbands to get married again, but most men prefer to stay single. It's hard to be a match-maker in Heaven. All you can do is steer people a certain way, and hope something happens. I suggest you tell Roger about certain women who would be good for him and let him take it from there."

"Should they have sex before marriage?" I asked him.

"Why not? Don't forget, sex was originally the method God used to make people be fruitful and multiply. Now, much to His consternation, they do it if there isn't anything good on TV."

"Is my idea correct that some women try to get a husband by shimmying between the sheets with him?"

"It's not unheard of. If a woman decides you're Mr. Right, then that's who you are."

Now that's metaphysical. After we left and were walking down the boardwalk, Bea said, "Moses is no help. I have a good prospect. I know a widow named Hilda Mermelstein who owns her own travel agency and gets to fly all over the world for nothing, and she's entitled to fifty-percent discounts on hotels. She's quite beautiful. Not as beautiful as you but she is not a hag, either. I know she's in the market for a husband. Tell Roger to go into the agency, inquire about a trip and maybe ask her for dinner. Hilda will go for it in a minute."

When I told Roger about her, I said she was one of our most attractive candidates. I described her in detail, including that Bea said she was a size six. Then I instructed him to go into her travel agency and have a look for himself. But over the next week whenever I asked him if he had seen Hilda, he said, "Not yet."

Finally the next weekend he reported that he'd had a date with her. It wasn't dinner but a Knicks game. Roger figured it wouldn't be a wasted evening if he could see the Knicks play.

I told Bea and she said, "I knew we could count on Hilda. She didn't even give any resistance about going to a basketball game, which I'm sure she had no interest in." For some reason, though, Roger said he didn't want to see Hilda again.

Roger's Story

I'm not going to tell Stella what happened on my date. Hilda said before the game she wanted to go to Bloomingdale's. But when she came out onto Lexington Avenue she had sunglasses in her bosom, perfume up her sleeves, and shoes under her coat.

"Did you pay for them?" I asked.

"Why should I? They owe me a lot more than this."

"Don't you think that makes you a kleptomaniac?"

"It's obvious this relationship is not working," she said and put her hand up for a cab.

"No, it isn't," I called to her. "You're a lovely lady but you have to start paying for things at Bloomingdale's or they're going to have a bad year."

I told Stella that Hilda and I didn't have the same chemistry. I said, "I like to give and she likes to take."

Stella's Story

I found Bea getting a simultaneous pedicure and manicure and gave her the news. She was disappointed. "I thought it would be the perfect match. Boy, you never know what attracts people these days. We're lucky we found out the chemistry wasn't there before real damage was done."

I told Bea, "Roger's so mad he hasn't talked to me in a week."

"He'll come back. With Sarah absorbed in her own problems, who else has he got to talk to?"

The next marriage prospect I thought of was my friend Lanie Myer. Lanie had been a divorcée for a long time. When I was alive all the wives in my circle were nervous when Lanie was in the room. The men would gather around her and while she maintained her innocence, we found out later there were dozens of fights in people's bedrooms about her after the party was over.

The reason I thought of Lanie is because she had no children. That might be a blessing to Roger with one on the way. Besides, Lanie had not lost her looks, especially after her two face-lifts.

Roger said he wasn't interested in another prospect. Also the word was out she preferred younger men.

I would have suggested Frances Rizzoli except she's not Jewish. I'm told Italian women make excellent wives. They're warm and they're good cooks, and I read in a book they're wonderful lovers. But I wasn't sure at this stage I could handle a *shiksa* as Roger's second wife.

Though she was helping me, Bea didn't like second wives. As she said, "Second wives get all the credit for the husband. The first wife is forgotten, in purgatory, if you will excuse the expression. Even at the funeral nobody mentions the first wife, the one who put her husband through school, who shared his poverty with him and who raised his children. She counts for zero. The second or third wife comes into the picture with a new hairstyle and everyone treats her like a movie star. Even at funerals the rabbi only mentions the second wife as the one everyone should pray for. No one talks about the first one.

"So much as I agree with you that it's a good idea for Roger to re-marry, if you find a wife, she'll be the one the congregation is asked to re-member, not you."

Bea's nails were under the dryer now.

I agreed. "There is something wrong with a system where they make the second wife the great motivator, and the first wife's name never is men-tioned again. Three years ago I was at Harlan Franklin's funeral. Four of his partners from his law firm said nice things about him. Each one said what a wonderful person Harlan's current and third wife, Rebecca, was too. No word on Frieda, the first one, who put Harlan through law school, no word about Betsy, who made a fortune for him in antiques. All they kept talking about was Rebecca, who was married to Harlan for three years and then got all the money.

"That's the main thing I'm worried about. If I get Roger another wife, everyone will forget me."

Bea tried not to move her hands and feet and said, "I hope they don't. You've put in so much time it would be a pity if some floozy took all the bows in the synagogue."

Bea treats me like a friend, Moses like my psy-chiatrist.

We left the salon, Bea's nails a deep red.

When Roger started talking again after the Hilda fiasco, he was filled with remorse and said he missed me. He apologized for getting angry and told me he was willing to let me continue the wife search provided I did not have a complete say as to who he would date. He said he was willing to listen. He told me that instead of finding a good fit, I should find someone who looked like Sophia Loren and cooked like Ava Gardner. I knew he was kidding. Roger jokes around a lot but ever since I passed away I'm onto his half-truths and he can't get away with much.

I told him this and Roger finally admitted his main problem was that he would feel disloyal if he fell in love with another woman. He said he would also feel bad if he married someone and didn't love her.

I wondered if there were any other women in Heaven who were looking for wives for their husbands. Mrs. Spingard admitted that she thought about it but did not have any communication with her Freddy. It didn't matter because the week after telling me this, Freddy met a widow on a cruise ship to Acapulco and had the captain marry them when they got out to sea. I asked her if this bothered her.

"No," she said. "The new wife works on the cruise ship and Freddy gets seasick very easily."

Roger's Story

Last night I called Stella and said, "Even though Sarah's pregnant she's hanging out with a weird bunch. One day she showed up with a Japanese fella who was shoeless and wearing a Star of

David. I didn't know what to make of it. After the sixties I can understand no shoes, but why's he wearing a Star of David?"

"Maybe he's Jewish. Or maybe he's one of Sarah's lost tribes."

We never did learn what faith her friend was. Timmy told me, "Don't get too upset, Dad. He could be the father of Sarah's child."

I wanted Stella to call off her wife search. It interfered with my social life, what little of it there was. Here I am on Earth, trying to figure everything out and Stella's in Heaven, drawing up blueprints for my next wife.

When I mentioned this to Stella, she said, "So don't talk to me. I don't want to spoil it for you when you're shimmying between the sheets."

"That's a good example. You're constantly accusing me of having an affair when you don't like what I say."

Stella's Story

I sensed Roger was changing and was no longer the man I had been married to. The next time we talked I changed the subject.

"What's going on with Timmy?"

"He's still happy with running the home in the Bronx for the disadvantaged kids. The court keeps asking him to take in more kids so they won't go to jail. He still doesn't have a girl since Judy Fleischer dumped him."

"Why did she dump him?"

"She said he couldn't make a real living, and do-gooders make bad husbands. You know, he hardly makes enough money to feed himself much less others. When he isn't working, he drops by when he can. I find his life sad, but after the war he still feels he has to do something."

Timmy hated the war, more than anyone I knew. I think my strongest memory of our kids is watching them disappear into a rally and not knowing if they would be back soon. But while they were protesting the war, Timmy's draft number came up.

We had talked about Timmy going to Canada if his number came up. Roger had problems with an American engaging in illegal acts against the government. All around us boys were being called up and those who had to send their sons were bitter about the protesters.

Timmy decided to go rather than take off for Canada. He said, "All my friends are being drafted. If I sit out the war while it's on, I wouldn't be able to live with myself after it was over."

With that, Timmy told us he was going.

I got all choked up and said, "Promise me you won't be a hero."

Rabbi Sparkman said to Roger and me, "It's the wrong decision but I think he's doing the right thing." Mimi said, "Those assholes in Washington think nothing about what they do with our flesh and blood."

Within a month Timmy was sent to Fort Dix to make a soldier out of him. He came back after a few months on leave. He looked good and seemed very confident.

"Not everyone goes to Vietnam, Mom," he told me. "They need soldiers in Korea and Germany and even Okinawa."

Then he went back to Fort Dix and the next thing we heard he was shipping out for Vietnam. He came home to say goodbye and we had Timmy's favorite meal: pot roast, red cabbage, baked potatoes and Key lime pie.

Roger said, "This is weird. We have one child going to Vietnam and another screaming for the downfall of the U.S. government. My mother pelts Henry Kissinger with eggs, while my son is expected to kill Communists."

There is something about saying goodbye to a child going off to war. I am not speaking now just as a mother. Timmy was such a good boy and had so much to give to his country and his community. It seemed such a waste to send him to a jungle 6,000 miles away to kill more people than could kill us.

In his letters he couldn't tell us where he was but he said he was in a company and had engaged in heavy fighting. He wrote that he lost his best friend, who'd stepped on a mine. Then he was sent to Saigon for leave.

When Sarah read this she said, "He's going to get the clap."

I got angry and said, "Timmy is too smart to have anything to do with Vietnamese prostitutes."

Mimi said, "After shooting them all month long you would think he wouldn't want to sleep with them."

The worst was when the news showed our troops walking through the jungle. Occasionally they displayed GI's carrying the dead and wounded. At one point we were certain we saw Timmy.

It also hurt when they showed Americans destroying the village of My Lai and we prayed and prayed that Timmy wasn't setting fire to villagers' huts.

One of the biggest fights I had was with Sylvia Mandelbaum. Sylvia was a rabid anti-war demonstrator. She came to the house to have us sign a petition for Nixon's impeachment. Of course Sarah signed it, then Mimi signed it. I was the only one who read it. It called Nixon a war criminal and said our soldiers over there were no better than Nazi SS troops.

I exploded, "Don't you call my son a Nazi!"

"I didn't say he was a Nazi. I said that he was no better than a Nazi."

I took all her signed petitions and tore them up. Sylvia screamed and grabbed my hair. I kicked her in the shins. Pretty soon we were rolling on the lawn. Roger came out and separated us. Sylvia gathered all the torn paper and cried, "I went door to door for a month to get all these signatures!"

I shouted, "My son is saving your ass, you Commie bitch!" I didn't really even know what a Communist was. Nobody did.

By this time the neighbors were all looking on. Whether they knew what was going on, most of them took my side because Sylvia never cut her lawn.

When I went back in the house, for the first time Mimi said, "I'm proud of you, Stella, for the way you stood up for my grandson."

"He also happens to be my son," I said.

Sarah said, "So what? He's my brother."

It was just an interlude but it did make me hate the war all the more.

Timmy was wounded on July 6th, 1971. We didn't hear about it until August 7th. The telegram failed to say how badly he was wounded or where. All it said was that he had been "flown to a hospital on Okinawa."

I wanted to go immediately to Okinawa, but Roger said he heard the army tried to get the men to Hawaii as soon as possible.

We found it impossible to get any information, then PFC William Cravath showed up at the door. He had served in Timmy's outfit and been sent home because his father had died. Timmy asked him to stop by and assure us that everything was okay.

We sat him in the living room and Roger

brought him a glass of milk and a piece of cheese-cake. He said Timmy had "caught it" (his term) at a village called Bi Minh. It looked unoccupied but when the men moved forward, the Viet Cong opened up on the platoon. The sergeant had been hit and Timmy went out to save him when they shot him in the leg. He dragged the sergeant back and afterwards the captain said he was going to get Timmy a medal besides the Purple Heart which he was already entitled to.

"How badly hurt is he?" Roger asked.

"He has problems walking on his wounded leg, but he's not going to die."

Mimi said, "Don't lie to us."

"I'm not lying. He was my buddy. He's going to be all right."

Then Mimi said, "Have you got a girl?"

Of course she had Sarah in mind, no matter how much Sarah was against the war.

"Yes, sir," the PFC replied.

"You don't have to call me sir," Mimi said, though you could tell she liked it.

Sarah and Mimi wanted to go to the hospital in Hawaii where Timmy was recuperating, but Roger talked them out of it. Roger said, "He wants to come back the way he was when he left us."

Timmy came home in time for Thanksgiving. Although he was wounded, Roger and I were relieved he was no longer in Vietnam. The doctor said he'd be able to walk normally within a year.

When Nixon resigned, Mimi went out into the

street banging a pan with a metal soup ladle. Sarah hung a homemade banner on the house which read "I am not a crook — Sure!" Everyone in the Folger family was happy about the resignation. With Tricky Dick out of office and Timmy home, we felt we could get on with our lives.

The waste was brought home to me years later when the family visited the Vietnam Memorial in Washington with its 58,196 names. Timmy recognized two of them and tears came to his eyes. We walked ahead and waited for him while he stroked his fingers over their names.

Roger went on to tell me more about the kids.

"Timmy misses you very much. You keep coming up in our conversations, particularly around Thanksgiving and Passover.

"The kids are okay. They're going through a few things of yours. Timmy picked up the surplus kitchenware and a few things from the living room for the kids in the Bronx. I remember buying most of it with you. Pictures that once brought me joy now cause sorrow. Almost everything we owned was chosen by both of us, except for the things selected by that weird decorator who stood en pointe when he was telling us what we needed.

"Stella, hardly anybody realizes how difficult it is to unload a lifetime of possessions. So many things in the house are there because you don't want to deal with getting rid of them. Everything

90

you refused to deal with in the past, you now must face up to. By getting rid of things you are acknowledging once again the terrible loss.

"I can't tell you how much I have wanted you by my side in the last month so I could say, 'What do you think we should do with your mother's quilt or these dresses in the back of the closet?' I don't even have the slightest idea how to get rid of the Kleenex box."

"You could give the stuff to your girlfriends."

"That's not funny, Stella. Look, if it bothers you I won't tell you anything about my social life."

"Why should I be bothered? I'm up here and you're down there. I'll tell you one thing, if I were down there, I'd hit you over the head with my wok. God's mistake is letting the wife go before the husband."

"You're being morbid now. This is the problem: when people are happily married they get on the same train and they go in the same direction. That's not life, it's their life. A reason they stick together is that it's easier for both of them. Also, they have a lot in common including aches and pains and history. The history is the most important. Now all of a sudden one of the two gets off the train and the other has no idea where it's going."

I was getting upset but figured Roger needed to get this off his chest.

"Then a whole world opens up, not a better world but a different one. The environment

91

changes. You meet different people, you react as if you're in your early twenties. You listen to women's stories. You come home at night exhausted. The phone is constantly ringing with people in trouble. When you were married, no one cared to tell you anything. Now they feel it's all right to unload on you. That's what happens because your role is no longer mapped out."

"So where do I fit in?"

"You'll always be part of my life. I'm talking to you now, so obviously I still care about you very much. Whenever something comes up I ask myself, I wonder what Stella would think of this? I always respected your ideas."

I never liked it when Roger got too mushy, so I asked about Sarah.

Roger sighed.

"Sarah is the one who hasn't adjusted at all. You were her enemy and now that you're gone she doesn't have one. I refuse to substitute for you. The other night she started in on me about not helping her make a decision about the baby and I said, 'You got the wrong person. I'm not going to be the heavy in your life.' She was furious.

"If you asked me what was the thing I miss the most about being with you, Stella, it's the meals we shared.

"People seem to pass their married lives in the kitchen. First a couple eats alone, then they eat with the children, every meal if they can. Then the kids start peeling off and pretty soon you're back to eating alone. Every celebration, whether Thanksgiving or Passover, became more and more important because it was the only time the kids came home. You were so happy bringing out the platters of brisket and chicken and red cabbage.

"And just when we thought we couldn't eat one more thing, you produced the finale: the pies. Pumpkin, Key lime and cherry with Breyer's ice cream, and everyone at the table groaned and laughed and said, 'Mom, when do we eat?' "

I was laughing now too. Roger continued.

"I think after those meals you were the happiest of all. It's when the holidays roll around that we miss you the most. The food in the kitchen, the joy on your face, the sense of family was all there. It really was.

"I don't accept dinner invitations like we used to do. How did we stand all these people for so many years, Stella, and why do they now drive me nuts? I get more pleasure out of helping people instead of drinking at parties.

"Stella, if I help more than one woman out of trouble am I doing anything wrong?"

I thought about it then said, "Maybe. Let's say a woman is interested in you. If you save her from drowning, she'll be ever grateful. But if you save the woman next to her, the first woman will never talk to you again. That's the way the world is and always has been."

"You're right. Women always get mad at me when I tell them I have other friends. This one lady was a CPA who worked on people's taxes. We were having coffee and I said how much I liked helping people out. She told me that if I were to continue seeing her, I would have to stop playing the good guy. I said how about if instead of personal charity, I give everything to her. She didn't like my sarcasm and that was the end of our relationship. The only thing that made me sorry about it was she told me she has access to her late husband's New York Giants tickets."

Roger's Story

If you were to ask me who was the most interesting woman I met after Stella passed away, it was Elena Gorschak. She was a rabbi. Rebecca and Ralph Markay had me over for dinner one night and didn't tell me they had arranged a blind date. I didn't even know Elena was a rabbi until the soup course. She was very good-looking, with reddish hair, and very smart. She said she had many men in her congregation who had lost their spouses and these men had no idea what was going on either.

I asked her what she counseled them and she said, "I tell them they don't have too many years left and they can either waste it or make a new life."

"I like that," I said. "I think Stella would tell me the same thing."

94

After this conversation I found myself going to temple on Friday night and Saturday morning. I realized it had more to do with the rabbi than the service. She wore a black velvet gown which impressed me very much and a cap almost like she was graduating from college.

I found out that she was forty-five years old, her ex-husband had run away with a female cantor, and she'd been hired by the temple when they could not find a male rabbi for the same price. Sarah and Timmy were shocked to hear I was emotionally involved with a forty-five-year-old rabbi.

At first Elena was reluctant to have anything to do with me. But when I went to one of her sermons and watched her do a number on Abraham, I told her afterwards I liked the way she looked when she conducted services, and she warmed up and let me see her home safely to Rego Park. My only concern was that Stella would be furious that I had taken up with a lady who made her living saying prayers and sermons, when I hadn't been that religious to start with.

The word was out in Forest Hills that I was courting a rabbi. This wasn't exactly true. We went to the movies and had supper afterwards at the Kew Rest. She claimed to be interested in my scientific work, as she knew people in the congregation who had herpes.

Twoey felt I was playing with fire. "I don't know much about your religion, but I am sure a female rabbi can make you more miserable than a male one. Rabbis and priests traffic in sin and guilt."

I didn't do anything we shouldn't have because you don't mess around with religious leaders. Once or twice we squeezed hands but that was it.

Stella finally heard about it through Prudin. She reacted in disbelief and then anger. She wanted to know if I was courting her and when I said no she asked, "Why a rabbi, anyway?"

"Why not a rabbi?" I said. "They need love too."

"You never even gave to the temple's building fund."

"I would think you would be happy that I have chosen such a chaste person."

"I wanted you to find someone but a woman rabbi is a little too much. You'll have no private life of your own. Everyone goes to the rabbi with his or her problems."

"You can't tell me who I can go with. All you can do is advise and consent."

Stella said, "We'll see."

I was getting definitely interested in Elena and preparing to make my next move. We'd just driven up in front of her apartment when she told me she had been offered a position in the Park View Congregation in Los Angeles. She would be the number-one rabbi as opposed to an assistant rabbi like she was in Forest Hills.

I threw caution to the wind and said, "How about I go with you?"

The car was stifling.

She turned to me and said, "Roger, I'm forty-five and you're sixty. That's just too much of an age difference for me."

It was the first time I realized I could be too old to have something I wanted.

I said, "When do you go?"

"Next week," she said. "For the High Holy Days."

She patted my hand and got out.

When I got back to Stella she said, "I hear she's gone. Maybe you should see a rabbi — a male one, this time."

Stella's Story

I know what you're wondering. Have I ever seen God? The answer is no. He keeps to Himself. I was told by a maid that He's afraid if He makes an appearance, everyone will ask for a favor. That's absolutely true. I know if God showed up at the pool I would ask Him to find a wife for Roger.

So I did the next best thing. I went down to the lobby, where I found Mary Magdalene and said, "Mary, since I left Roger and he didn't leave me, I feel obligated to find him someone who will make him happy. Do you think there's anything wrong with my searching for a wife for him?"

She said, "What kind of woman are you trying to find for him?"

97

"I have some good candidates. Women that Roger would adore."

"No one up here can help you. You have to have a real reason for Divine intervention, and finding another woman for your husband is not a strong enough reason."

This left me on my own. The search was far more complicated than I thought it would be. I had a problem. If I selected someone with impeccable credentials like Margie Bernheim, who had fresh flowers delivered by Kottmiller Florists for her living room every day, it would be trouble. Margie was the perfectionist of the neighborhood. She did everything right and was attractive, though the rumor at the beauty parlor was she took four years off her age on her passport. I never repeated this of course.

My concern was Margie, being perfect, might make me look like a *schlub*. And Roger might feel like he wasted all that time with me when he could have had Margie instead. I crossed her name off the list.

Inez Hyman lost her husband two years ago, about the same time Roger lost me. I haven't run into her husband up here. He sold used cars so I don't know if he made it to Heaven. He certainly isn't on the main campus.

There are good things and bad things about Inez when it comes to Roger. She has a mind of her own, something Roger could use, and she's always telling other people what to do. By the same token, she's High Maintenance. She owns a place in Tanglewood, where she goes in the summer and attends all the concerts. Roger would automatically like anyone who owns a place in the Berkshires. But she is a snob and that makes Roger very insecure. I don't think I would be doing him a good turn by arranging something between him and Inez. I'm keeping her on the list for the moment.

When it comes to women, and I'm the only exception, Roger has no great taste.

Okay, I'll tell you the truth. While I'd like to find Roger a wife for his sake, what I'm most worried about is that people will forget me. It's the major concern of everyone up here. You can have everything you want, but nothing can be done about the hold your family once had on you.

In fact, the thing we talk the most about in Heaven is our lives on Earth. Some people maintain they had had rotten lives, others that everything had been good. Strangely, those who had had unhappy lives on Earth are still unhappy in Heaven. Their beds are too hard or too soft, the hot tub is too hot or it isn't hot enough, they don't like the Muzak piped into Heaven.

My friend Miriam Freedman is a good example. She had a very unhappy childhood. Her mother put her in a foster home and ran off with the milk driver. Her foster parents turned her into a servant. Miriam did the laundry, the ironing and cleaning. Miriam told me I was one of the few people she talked to. She had such lack of self-esteem that when she grew up, she married a compulsive gambler who lost all his money betting on feeble horses at the racetrack.

"I never thought I deserved anything better," she said.

So she came to Heaven with all her baggage and cannot enjoy the wonderful things offered. I thought it was unfair for people to come to Heaven when they didn't have the ability to enjoy it.

There is one person, Bob Novack, who's constantly complaining about the movies we show. He's a Joan Crawford fan and for some reason has developed a terrible dislike for Esther Williams. He keeps telling us at dinner that Heaven is poorly managed because they don't know what classic movies to show.

According to the rules, we're not permitted to have rancor toward a chronic complainer and that is what drives us all crazy. If you have to swallow anger, it gets to your stomach and you have to take Rolaids.

One time I sat at Moses' table and I posed the question to him. "Why do you take in so many unhappy people when they can't have a good time here?"

While munching on Cheerios, Moses said, "Heaven is for everybody, the happy and the unhappy. God doesn't discriminate between people based on their mood swings."

"Maybe unhappy people coming to Heaven should be given Prozac."

"God doesn't believe in giving people mood-swinging drugs when they are down."

"Why not?"

"Because Heaven wouldn't be Heaven if people started taking pills. Your friends will eventually get over their unhappy childhoods."

"How?"

"Hot balsam baths. If anyone sounds depressed, send them to the spa and one of our angels will make them feel better."

The most wonderful thing about Moses is that he always has time to talk to you. By the way, he doesn't look anything like Charlton Heston. The real Moses is so much better-looking and is clean shaven. Bea says he looks like a teddy bear.

The last few times I talked to Roger he was upset. Sarah wasn't certain if she wanted the baby or not. Roger wanted her to have it and said he would raise the child if he had to.

His reason for wanting her to have it wasn't the best one. He said, "Maybe this will make a woman out of her."

"Roger, you don't have to have children to become a woman."

"Okay, okay," he said. "Stella, I want her to have the child, but I sure don't see myself as a doting grandfather."

"What does Timmy say?"

"You know Timmy. He told Sarah to have the baby and everything would be all right. In his job he sees a lot of unwanted pregnancies turn out all right."

"I don't like Sarah having a baby without me being there," I told Bea afterwards.

"She doesn't sound like she can handle it, Stella. But then you never know when a woman gives birth. It changes her. She realizes that she's not the only person on Earth. My daughter was a lot like your Sarah. She spent her nights in discos and days waiting on tables at the Red Frog. One day she discovered she was going to have a child by the Hungarian chef. I said I would support her if she had the baby. The father of the baby said he would support her if she didn't. Well, she had the child, the chef proposed to her, and they now own a French restaurant in Palm Beach called Au Revoir Victor."

The reports on Sarah kept coming in from Roger. One day she was going to marry a man who was not the father but loved her and volunteered for the role; the next day she was going to go to the abortion clinic to sign up.

Roger sounded desperate. "I have no idea what to do. Help me, Stella."

I ran into Moses in the bowling alley. As usual he bowled a perfect score.

I told him what was going on. St. Peter sat next to him.

Moses said, "It seems to me I've heard this story before. The trouble is women let men have their pleasure, but there is a price to pay." He rolled another bowling ball, then gave his final thought: "Because we believe in propagating the human race we always advise the woman to have the child."

I told Roger what Moses said.

"We don't have any say about it, Stella. Sarah got mad at me last night because I said she was a disgrace to you, and she said she never wanted to see me again. The problem is that Sarah is not ready for motherhood. I don't think she will be for another twenty-five years."

Originally, Roger's news had come as a shock to me. It should not have because I knew Sarah was having affairs. Once I asked her if she used any precaution and she said, "I just think of England."

Bea told me it wasn't my business anymore.

"Then it's Roger's business," I said. "If she has the child, someone is going to have to support her. I knew Sarah would drive me crazy even when I got to Heaven but I didn't know how she would do it."

Bea said, "I hope she wants the baby. I'm a very liberal person and I have always been pro-choice, but when it comes down to it, I want the baby to be born. Does that make me a hypo-crite?"

I said I didn't think so. If I were on Earth I would support pro-choice for Sarah as long as she had the baby.

Mary Magdalene was arranging flowers in the lobby. I told her what was going on. I'm always amazed how she can listen to everyone's story and also take such good care of the Ritz.

She was reassuring, as usual. "Many women

who become pregnant do not look like they can handle a pregnancy. But somehow they do. It comes naturally to them. Once they see and hold the baby, they know what to do."

"Is God responsible for making them that way?"

"He's responsible for everything, but He takes special pleasure in bringing newborns to Earth. Sarah is not only dealing with the child inside her but also the fact that she must now grow up, and my guess is she doesn't like it."

"What should I do?"

"There is not much you can do except possibly give Roger support. Men are very frightened when it comes to birth. In a sense it does not have anything to do with them."

St. Peter, who was scribbling notes, said, "You're going too fast."

I said to Moses, "What do you do with all the notes Saint Peter takes?"

"We keep them in the files. It's impossible to remember everything everybody has talked about so the files help. I don't know what I'd do without Saint Peter."

Moses told me that there is just so much anyone can do from Heaven when it comes to people still on Earth. "They have to resolve their own problems or they won't take responsibility for them. If Sarah decides to have her baby, she'll turn out to be a good mother, you'll see. If we do it for her, she might never take an interest in the child. I admire you very much, Stella, but you do like to control everything, here and on Earth."

I got the impression Moses was chastising me. This worried me because I didn't want to get on his bad side. If you get on the wrong side of Moses up here, you can get yourself into a heap of trouble, like being assigned a room over-looking the golf-cart garage instead of the ocean.

I told Roger that Moses informed me the baby was Sarah's decision. Roger said, "Did Moses tell you what I was supposed to do with the baby once it's born?"

I told him Moses said, "Things will work out. They always do."

I won't say when I was alive that I was a great mother or a poor one. I was called a perfectionist because I liked everything clean. All my friends used to say, "Stella, you have such a clean house. What is your secret?" I would say, "I don't have a secret. I just like everything the way it should be. It's my problem if I hate dust. My mother was like this; Sarah, my daughter, is the oppo-site. The genes in our family only went just so far."

Early in our marriage Roger's mother used to come over to the house on military inspection tours. She was very disappointed when she could not find any dust. She gave up after a while and decided that her son had married below him for a dozen other reasons.

I wouldn't be thinking about it now except that my vision of Sarah, who couldn't fit a pillow into a pillow case, was bleak when it came to taking care of a baby.

I recall when I gave birth to my own children. Timmy was first, Sarah was second. Father and Mother were at the hospital for Timmy's birth. Roger said that both my parents kept looking at him in the waiting room with hostility, as if he had done something wrong. My mother said, "I thought you weren't going to have children for the first three years," to which Roger replied, "The condom broke and Stella conceived."

Then my father barked, "Now see what you did?"

Roger asked, "What did I do?" and Mother said, "If anything happens to Stella we'll never forgive you."

Roger told them, "She's going to have a wonderful baby and you are going to be very proud grandparents."

The kvetching would have continued but the nurse came out at that moment and said, "It's a beautiful baby boy." The three of them jumped up and kissed and hugged each other.

I saw Baby Timmy a little later and he cuddled right up to me — I was so happy. Mother said, "I'll be there when you want me because Roger probably can't afford help." Father said, "The first thing we have to do is get an endowment policy for him. Colleges now cost an arm and a leg."

Sarah came two years later. Roger was happy

our second child was a girl and gave Mother the go-ahead to fix up the second bedroom.

Timmy was also excited about a new sister. He piled up all his toys for her and Roger said he kept looking out the window for our arrival.

Once Sarah was home we were a happy family except that she yelled her head off from the moment we put her in a crib. She seemed hungry for my breast all the time. As time went on, Roger was the childrearing philosopher and I became the driver. I drove them to school, I drove them to tennis lessons, I drove them to soccer games and later to dances. I swear, I don't recall not being behind the wheel when they were kids.

Once when things got really bad we went to family therapy. The four of us got in our car and went to Dr. Lenz's house. Now, Roger didn't like family therapy because it took his mask away. He never wanted other people knowing what he was really thinking.

My lasting memory of the doctor's office is Sarah and me sitting as far apart as we could while Roger and Timmy held their heads in their hands. Nothing came of the sessions except on the way home each of us accused the other of betrayal.

The sixties was a difficult period for parents and children. It's a time that sticks out in my mind more than all the other good things that happened to our family.

Roger's Story

The big day arrived last week. I was feeding my rats purified water when Carol Rial, my assistant, came in and said, "It's Timmy at the hospital. He says Sarah's just given birth to a boy!"

I dashed out in my white coat, hailed a taxi. "I'm a doctor," I told the driver. "Take me to Mount Sinai Hospital."

When I got there Timmy was waiting. "Everything is fine. She told the nurse she's going to name the baby Gregory." Someone next to us said, "What's the father's name?"

I said, "I don't know, but I'd love it if you could find out."

We took Sarah and Gregory home. She said she wasn't sure whether she wanted to keep him.

I was angry and said, "The baby stays right here."

What had me worried was that Sarah, while not sure about Gregory, was still concerned about saving elephants from poaching in Uganda. This was the time when I really needed Stella.

I called her. "I wasn't going to have a nurse in the house, but I need someone who has had experience with infants. I was never good with Sarah and Timmy when they were babies."

She said, "I'll find a solution in Heaven. Don't do anything until you hear from me." I couldn't wait more than a day, however, and I hired Miss Samantha Arnaud from the Forest Hills Cradle Agency.

Miss Arnaud came from Wales and is in her early forties. Her last reference is from Mrs. MacTyler in Woodmere, Long Island, who said Samantha had been loving with her Orville and did her duties without complaint. I liked the last part. A quiet nurse is hard to find. They sold me when they said she is a great skier, which is rare in nannies. She was neat but not a fanatic. They said she had a lovely voice when she sang Orville to sleep.

My next question was why she was leaving. Mrs. MacTyler said they were moving to Arizona and Samantha was allergic to horses. I figured with us in Queens that wouldn't be a problem.

In her first interview with me, Samantha showed her humor when she said, "I imagine you were expecting Deborah Kerr." I liked the idea she had seen *The King and I* and was therefore educated. She is also very attractive and has a sense of humor. She has blonde hair and a twinkle in her eye. There's something about her that makes you know that she can handle any child and any child's mother, and maybe even any child's grandfather.

While I was sizing her up, she was sizing me up. She told me later on that she would never work for anyone she doesn't like. There are some people who blame a nanny for everything.

I told her I didn't know what to ask her as I had never hired a nanny before, so we went upstairs to the baby's room. Gregory started to cry. But when Samantha picked him up and held him in her arms, he quieted right down.

At this moment Sarah and Mimi came into the room. Sarah said, "What are you doing with my kid?"

Mimi said, "And my grandkid."

I said, "This is Gregory's nurse."

Mimi and Sarah looked at each other and back at me. "Why does he need a nurse?"

"So you will be free to throw eggs at the White House."

Samantha handed the baby to Sarah and said, "Don't worry. He'll always be yours."

And that's how Samantha has come into our lives. If I have anything to criticize about her, it's that she always keeps the washing machine going. Stella would have hated her.

Gregory takes a great deal of my attention. First there was the bris. After it was over I asked the rabbi, "Which Jewish prophet came up with the idea of circumcising a baby?"

You know what he said? "I don't know."

So all of a sudden Stella and I were like parents again, and Gregory has a grandmother on Earth and one in Heaven.

Four weeks have gone by and Gregory is interfering with my social life. In fact, not only do I have a kid at home again, I've even tried dating a few women with children. I guess I thought we would be able to share our trials.

One night I went with a lady to a black-tie affair for a big pharmaceutical company. It happened to be the same evening her boy had a hockey game. The mother chose to go out with me and the kid has never let her forget it. Women have a difficult time going out when the kids spread their bodies across the door.

There was another nice woman named Esther Shapiro who has two preteen children. We went out on dates as a foursome. I was never with her alone. The kids were always hitting each other in the restaurant and making faces at people at other tables. Several times other customers stopped by and said to us, "You should know better how to take care of those brats." I could never explain that they didn't belong to me.

Then Twoey tried to be the big fixer again. He said he had found me a date with a divorced biology professor from Swarthmore, Natasha Kleinwasser. The catch was, she said she liked to meet all her men for the first time at the New York Public Library. Twoey took us to the cafeteria for coffee. After a second cup she asked me if I wanted to go to the opera *La Bohème*. I decided it was a better thing to do than sit at home. I also decided the less Stella knew about it the happier the date would be for me. I used to refuse to go to the opera with Stella, so she'd smell a rat. She also knew I didn't like biology professors, so she might wonder what the attraction was. The attraction was that it was one of Twoey's women.

I met Natasha in the lobby of Lincoln Center. She told me she'd be wearing a red dress and a diamond brooch of a swan. We sized each other up and then went into the opera house.

"Did you bring your opera glasses?" she asked.

"Damn," I said, "I forgot them. I can't remember anything anymore."

As soon as we were seated she said, "My former husband was forgetful, and a son of a bitch too."

I wasn't too sure what the correct response was to that.

Just before the curtain went up she sighed, "All men are bastards."

"Even those who go to the opera with you?"

"You'll turn out to be a bastard too."

"What are we doing here, then?"

"I had an extra ticket and I didn't want to go alone."

After *La Bohème*, at which she cried more than I expected, we went to Mooch Lee for dinner.

This is the part of dates that I hate. Your date wants to know where you went to school, and you're supposed to ask where she went to school. If you went to school with George Stevens from Great Neck by chance, she will trust you more.

I finally took her home. She said, "I don't

want to sleep together."

"I had no intention of it."

She got angry and said, "Why not?"

It's scenes like this that make you swear you'll never go out on a date again.

Stella later asked, "How was *La Bohème*?"

"What do you know about that?"

"Prudin said the late owner of the Mooshie Lee Restaurant who lives in Suite 234 told her you were there."

"It was lousy. The woman, Natasha, found out about Gregory and told me she wasn't interested at her age in raising a child. She wasn't even nice about it and canceled our date to see *Carmen*."

"Why are you going out with someone who likes opera and who hates children?"

"She doesn't hate children. She's a very nice woman who likes music but doesn't like babies."

Stella's Story

I shouldn't have shown Roger how upset I was. In fact, I didn't understand why I was so angry since we're not supposed to get so upset here.

I asked Prudin about this Natasha woman. She was happy to give me bad news. It turns out she had been married twice. She had two children who were grown up and were both divorced. She liked to twist men around her finger. The worst part Prudin told me is that her files indicate she gets massages every day. I never trust a woman who's so relaxed. Prudin said that none of her ex-husbands spoke highly of her.

Bea warned me that I would get depressed in Heaven if I kept worrying about what Roger was up to. "You have to give him space," she said. "If you try to run his life now, he will hate you. Roger's no stud. Besides, he's just become a grandfather. How much trouble can he get into?"

Bea said my problem was jealousy, not guilt over leaving Roger alone. I kept telling everyone I believed Roger should have a life. But it was obvious I didn't want him to have one that would do psychic damage to mine.

Yesterday when Moses was playfully spraying Evian water on everyone by the pool, I asked him, "Moses, why do people start fooling around as soon as their spouses go to Heaven?"

Moses said, "No one likes to be lonely. When someone loses their spouse, the only way they can survive it is by finding somebody else. If someone finds another mate that they can live with, they're very lucky. Women, by the way, are better at it than men."

"I don't want Roger to be lonely, Moses. At the same time, I don't trust the women he's hanging out with."

"Why not?"

"They're all blondes."

"Didn't you say that's what you wanted for

114

Roger?" Moses shook his head. "God wouldn't want you to like someone or dislike them based on the color of their hair. I don't believe it's a good idea to interfere with Roger now. You might frighten him into finding the wrong companion. At some point you'll have to give him up, Stella. The person you were attached to is not yours anymore. It isn't easy because you know so much about him, you can't stand the idea of another woman finding out the same things about him, even touching him. But Roger has to continue his life, and this means without you."

I couldn't believe that both Bea and Moses had turned against me.

Roger's Story

Stella kept badgering me about a wife. I told her, "Every woman I've gone out with has one or two excellent features but six or seven drawbacks. I haven't turned into a womanizer. I'm just looking for companionship and someone to talk to. It's not easy."

There's one lady I met on my own who's very nice but she's in therapy and goes to her shrink every day.

On our first date, to her gym, Lola asked if I took Prozac, Zoloft or Paxil. When I said none of the above she was disappointed. When we were on the treadmill, she told me she loved her father and hated her mother but was on the fence about her sister, though early in life she hated her also. By the time we'd run three miles and I was gasping for breath, she said she found me a very good listener for someone who was not in therapy and was hoping we could develop a decent relationship in which one person respected the other while, at the same time, they were both guaranteed space.

I had no idea how to get rid of her. The next time she called, I was soaking my muscles in the tub, still trying to recover days later. She asked me if I would like to go to a lecture titled "Self-Abuse — What's the Answer?" Like a *schlemmiel* I went and afterwards, while walking in the rain, she revealed that as a child she masturbated twice a week while thinking of Errol Flynn. I told her that it wasn't necessary to tell me too many details about herself, and she said if we were going to have a relationship, I had to know everything about her. I said I wasn't sure I wanted to know everything.

She said, "I never want to speak to you again" and stalked off for a midnight ride on the A train.

Three days later she called back and said, "How come you haven't called me?"

Twoey thought I needed some "real" excitement in my life. After the analysand, he introduced me to a female lawyer who had been married to a stockbroker. The first thing she wanted to know was my sign. She told me her last husband's sign, Aries, was very wrong for her and she had no intention of making the mistake again. I told her I was a Libra and passed the test. The conversation continued to be unnerving as the lady was a divorce lawyer exclusively representing women. Over drinks in the Village she told me, "I specialize in emasculating the husbands of my clients until there is nothing left of their private parts."

I told her how much I admired someone who did that for a living. At the end of the evening she told me she'd like to see me again as we seemed to have so much in common. I didn't like the idea since she kept looking down at my private parts.

The expectations are high on the first date. Each person has dressed up as sharp as possible and is on his or her best behavior. The conversation is idiotic but you're examining for potential. After the third date the cracks start to show, and the differences in personalities become glaring. "Is that the only tie you own?" "I don't approve of smoking." "I hate people who eat garlic."

Twoey's blind dates are something else entirely. It's not easy to talk to them for any length of time. Most of Twoey's dates are thirty-five and under. You can have a three-minute conversation on any subject as long as the subject is Madonna or Michael Jackson.

If Twoey wasn't so insistent, I'd stay in bed.

Stella was not just curious about little Gregory, she also asked about everyone I was seeing. "What are they like?" she would say.

117

"Come on, tell me!"

"They're nothing compared to you. You spoiled me."

She said, "Even if that isn't true, I believe you."

"I think a lot about our marriage now. You provided me with things I needed, and I provided you with things you needed. I hope, anyway."

She ignored the last.

"What did I provide you, Roger?"

"Wisdom. I never have been too smart about life, and you seemed to always have the answers."

"Well, you did pretty well for somebody who wasn't too sure of himself."

"Besides everything else, you provided me with a good sex life. I wouldn't have said this before but now I realize we made wonderful love. I always looked forward to it."

"That's nice of you to say, Roger. You were a good lover too. You were never boring in bed. Sex is very important in a marriage. If it's good, you're always looking forward to it. If it's no good, the person you're with starts to look very uninteresting."

"Why do you think we were so good in bed?"

"Because we loved each other and wanted to give each other a gift. We learned what pleased the other person and by doing what pleased each other both were satisfied. Roger, I don't know whether we should be talking about sex while

I'm in Heaven. Either that or we're going to have to "

"God wouldn't let us have sex if it weren't okay."

Things were heating up like they used to.

"So have you found any woman that satisfies you in bed?" she had to ask.

So much for phone sex. "That's a dumb question and I'm not going to answer it. Sex is not something women give lightly. When a woman gives it she wants something in return."

"How do you know?"

I slowed down and tried to be nicer.

"Sophia Loren told me. I think sex means a lot more to women than it does to men. When a woman has been with a man for a long time and then loses him, she's not sure whether she wants to have another sex partner. A man, on the other hand, feels liberated and wants to make love to everything he sees."

"Sarah would say you're being a sexist."

"Sexist or no, that's the way I see things."

"Does Minnie Goldberg come sniffing around?"

"She was the first to try. I never let her in the house because she would never leave."

"I should have warned you about her. When I was dying, she told Audrey that she was going to rope you as soon as I got out of the picture. Audrey said she was furious with Minnie since I was still alive at the time. But all Minnie said was she didn't have much time either."

I said, "Minnie's not my type anyway. The truth is, she's a big pain in the ass and you never heard me say one nice thing about her."

She agreed. "The man who gets her is not going to enjoy his September years." Then she said, "One of your problems is that you don't stay busy."

I told her, "I take care of Gregory on the weekend sometimes. But it's true, most of the time when I'm not working, I just sit and think. I am reading a piece on high blood pressure in the *New England Medical Journal*, but I know I should be thinking about herpes."

Stella's Story

I know this sounds crazy, but even in Heaven I miss the beach on Long Island where Roger and I went with the family in the summertime. Mother and Father had two cabanas next to each other and we would drive out in the morning and if the weather was nice, we'd stay all day. The women crocheted and the men played gin rummy.

Mimi went with us under duress and made snide remarks about everyone. That is, until she met Mr. Sy White. Mr. White was a silver-haired divorcé who owned forty movie theaters in Brooklyn. He was seventy years old and asked Mimi to go to one of his movie theaters where he was showing *Love in the Afternoon*. The whole

120

family encouraged her. I hoped it would be a break for me.

Mimi even bought a dress for her date, she was so excited. She returned at one o'clock in the morning. We were all sitting in the living room back in Queens, waiting for a report.

"So?"

"He doesn't sell real butter on his popcorn."

I, who had the most to gain, asked, "But do you like him?"

Mimi said, "He's okay. He likes money."

I said, "What's wrong with that?"

Mimi just shrugged and drifted off to bed.

It seemed serious for a while until the day Mimi asked Mr. White to unionize his ushers so they could get better wages. This didn't go over very well with him, particularly since Mimi also accused him of using child labor. So Mr. White stopped calling and we lost our "Great White Hope."

Roger's Story

Twoey came to visit me at the lab, which was very unusual for him. He hung around, watching me clean out the cages. I knew something was wrong, but assumed it had to do with one of his girl-friends.

"I need $50,000," he said.

"Twoey, I don't have $50,000. You lost all my

money in an oil dump."

"That's my point. The only way I can get it back for you is to build more houses. What about a mortgage on your house?"

I stopped my work and said, "Twoey, you know I would do anything in the world for you, but my house belonged to Stella and me and I would hate to mortgage it and she would hate it too."

"She's dead."

"I know but she'd find out some way."

Twoey didn't know what I was talking about and it was best he didn't.

Twoey took out a calculator and multiplied fifty times two and proved that $50,000 could become $100,000 in no time and with capital gains. He hit the calculator several times more, proving I could make $250,000 in two years.

The outcome of the conversation was I got a mortgage on the house. Twoey convinced me it was the only sure way of getting Stella's insurance money back.

My problem is I've never been good with money. When Stella's windfall arrived it was more money than I knew what to do with. I had never had $150,000 before. I hadn't even thought about it until they sent me the check. When it arrived I thought God was trying to make up for taking Stella away.

Now I had one fear and that was that Stella would hear about the mortgage and never forgive me.

Stella's Story

Something terrible happened. Roger told me Gregory was taken to hospital with pneumonia. I didn't even know that babies could get pneumonia until Dr. Lovell, who is up here in Room 645 and is an obstetrician, said that if the situation didn't improve the baby could die.

Roger was crying when he told me about Gregory.

"He's such a little fellow," he said. "He can't fight this battle on his own."

After what Dr. Lovell told me, I panicked. Bea had to hold me down I was so hysterical. She said, "Go see Moses. Maybe he can help this time. God isn't going to let a little baby die."

I found Moses fertilizing his rose garden. "I'm known for burning bushes when, in fact, my specialty is growing roses," he said.

"No jokes, Moses. I have a dying baby and I want to see God."

Moses turned to me with raised eyebrows. "You can't see God."

"Why not?"

"Because everyone has someone dying in their family. God can't hear all their appeals."

"I just want Him to hear mine. He can't take a six-month-old baby away from my family."

Moses was firm. "God won't see you," he said and he went back to the garden.

"So what do I do?"

"Maybe you could write Him a letter."

"God reads letters?"

"If they're written in good taste. He doesn't like bad language or people cursing at Him for something that is their fault."

I went back to my room. Bea was waiting. "So? What did he say?"

"He said I should write a letter to God and make my case. You have to help me, Bea. This is the most important letter I've ever written in my life."

Bea said this was the first she had heard of writing to God. "Most people pray to Him."

"Praying doesn't work up here. How should I start the letter?"

" 'Your Holiness'?"

"That's for the Pope, not for God. How about 'Dear Lord' or 'Dear Jaweh,' or 'Heavenly Father'?"

"Any of those will do. Tell Him how much you like it up here and how you personally want to thank Him for everything He and Moses, Mary Magdalene and Saint Peter have done for us."

"He'll go for that. Even God likes to be appreciated for what He does. But I want to get down to business before He loses interest."

An hour later I had come up with a letter and I read it aloud to Bea:

"Dear God,
    Gregory Folger is just a tiny baby and

hasn't done anything to anybody. Please don't take him away from his family, especially my Roger who already suffered a loss when I died two years ago. I guarantee if You spare him he will grow up to be a wonderful person and serve You as well as the human race just as You would want him to. We were going to abort him but we chose to have him instead, so what sense is there to take him from us now?"

Bea was in tears. She said, "God has to be moved by your letter, even if He gets a thousand requests every day."

"Should I tell Him I am the grandmother of the child?"

"God knows that. He knows everything."

I found a beautiful envelope in the gift shop with angels all over it and gave it to St. Peter to give to God. "Hand delivered," I insisted.

When St. Peter saw the address he was shocked. He checked it out with Moses, who said it was all right to deliver it, but not to make a big deal about it because it would produce a flood of mail.

That night Roger asked a bit angrily, "Who decides who goes to Heaven, anyway?"

"I think it's done by an admissions committee like at Harvard. The members have all the facts and they decide on people as they would for a co-op apartment. I hardly want to think about it right now."

"Doesn't God have anything to say?"

"I guess He can't make a decision on everyone who dies. He makes the laws and runs Heaven and Earth and every place else. But He doesn't like to get involved if someone starts a fight over a person taking someone else's parking place, for example. I've never seen God but Bea says she did one day when He was playing croquet. Of course I don't believe her. God doesn't play croquet with His subjects."

Roger asked me if there were any children up here. There are but they have a special wing next to the badminton court. They have the run of the place except for the pool area, which is strictly reserved for adults. The children have their own pool and Tarzan is the lifeguard. The men, on the other hand, are mostly involved with poker and backgammon games, even though they know they're not permitted to play for money. The women do not have a lot to do with the men because most of them have had experience with them on Earth.

"Why does God take children?" Roger asked. His voice was cracking.

"We're not allowed to ask. Bea thinks God has a giant computer like the phone company and every day it spits out names. It's already programmed."

"Frankly, I think Bea doesn't know what she is talking about," Roger said.

Roger got me so nervous that I decided I'd better use my second wish. I wished that

Gregory would recover by the end of the week.

A few days later I heard from Roger that the baby was recovering and the doctors were amazed how fast his temperature had gone down. I didn't know whether the letter or the wish did the trick. I also didn't tell Roger what I had done because he would have told everyone and then they'd know about our phone line. As it is, Rabbi Sparkman took full credit for the miracle and told Roger, "I do very well with prayers."

Roger's Story

Mimi has acquired a new boyfriend. His name is Saul Nuddleman and she met him at a Senior Citizens' hop in the basement of our temple which is reserved on Monday nights. He's a widower and a retired optometrist. Mimi asked him to dance. During the dance she discovered his blood pressure is 120/80 and he doesn't smoke. He has his own teeth and a nice income from investments in a box factory on Staten Island. Mimi suggested he drive her home, even though she had her own car in the parking lot.

According to her story, when they got to her house she asked, "Do you want to kiss me?"

He said he didn't know.

"You can kiss me but we can't fool around," Mimi told him. "We have to get to know each other better. Call me tomorrow."

That's how the romance started and Saul has been at the dinner table every night since then. He never says much. Mimi speaks for him. Whenever I ask him a question, either about politics or optometry, Mimi pipes up and says, "Saul was always a Democrat. He even hated Eisenhower" or "Saul hates the idea that people can buy eyeglasses in drug stores."

Sarah was slightly put out that Mimi was spending more time with Saul than she was with her and Gregory, so she decided to tag along whenever they went out. This has left me and Samantha to do the babysitting.

There was no talk with Stella for a while about the women in my life because I never had time to go out. In fact, she seemed to have backed off for some reason and I wasn't about to ask why. But since I was home so much we had more time to talk.

"Where do Mimi, Saul and Sarah go?"

"Rock concerts, scary movies and the 92nd Street Y when they have nothing else to do," I said. "I'm not too sure that this is Saul's bag, but he doesn't say anything. Mimi tells him what he's to do and he does it."

"Does Mimi say they're serious?"

"Saul doesn't seem to have much choice in the matter. Mimi's thinking of taking a cruise to Alaska, but she says if she goes, Saul has to bring Sarah and the baby. I'm all for it. I need a rest."

"What about Timmy? Does he have a new girl yet?"

"I don't think so. He was so badly burned by

Judy dumping him that he doesn't seem to want to date. Unlike Judy, several women think he would make a good catch even if he hardly makes a living. But Timmy is devoted to his work. There are so many kids in the Bronx who don't have fathers or mothers. They love Timmy. I saw it with my own eyes when he took me up there.

" 'Timmy,' I said. 'These kids really care for you,' and he said with a grin, 'I'd make a great father.'

" 'What's in it for you?' I asked him.

" 'They know I get how hurt they are and they know someone is there.' "

Stella's Story

Bea and I started to put our heads together as time was running out for our wife search. Roger was occupied with the baby, Sarah and Mimi. I could tell from talking to him that he was unraveling.

Bea said it best: "He's ripe to take any woman he can get at this moment. But you can't let him get stuck with anybody just because she looks better than his situation without a woman."

I said, "If we don't find someone, who will?"

Bea said, "I know a woman, a divorcée named Martha Lanham. She's fifty years old and still very attractive with an ample bosom, which you told me is what Roger likes. She has two grown-up children, one making a bundle on Wall Street and one, her daughter, is a doctor. She would not be coming to Roger as a welfare case."

"Where does she live?"

"Scarsdale."

"Is she smart?"

"Sure she is. She won't bore Roger. The only thing wrong with her is that she's a take-charge lady. She likes to run everyone's life, and the trick is that she doesn't let on she's doing it."

"Why did she get divorced?"

"I think her husband got sick of her. The way she tells it, he was fooling around with a woman who was installing software on his computers at his house. Martha's husband was coming home later and later until Martha found a love letter in her husband's in-basket. That was enough and she kicked him and his computers out."

"She sounds interesting, but I don't want it to be too obvious I had a hand in it. Even if Roger went for her, I would want him to believe it was his choice."

Bea said, "I know. Tell Roger to ask for Martha in her antique store on Third Avenue and 54th Street and have him say you bought something there when you were alive and never got to pick it up. Use my name as a reference."

"That doesn't sound like it'll work."

"Believe me, it will work. When she discovers Roger's a widower, she will do the rest."

"Maybe she's too forward."

"We're desperate. What are our choices?"

I wasn't confident it would work. That night I told Roger, "I want you to go to an antique store. I bought a plate there they never delivered. The owner's name is Martha and she specializes in the Ming Dynasty. Bea knows her too."

A few days later I asked him if he had stopped by the store.

"Yes. I asked for your plate and I didn't understand why she started trying to sell me an end table for $60,000. Then we got into a fight because she said I was not supposed to pick up anything in the store. She wanted to know how I knew about her, and I was stuck because I couldn't tell her we talk to each other almost every night and I couldn't think of Bea's name. So I walked out of the shop without saying anything.

"A few days later I got a call from her and she asked me if I wanted to go to a friend's wedding with her."

When I told Bea that Roger had a date she said, "That's my Martha." So as far as I knew, Martha and Roger were dating, though he wasn't talking about it. Bea said not to tip my hand because I could wreck the romance.

But I couldn't keep quiet. "How are you doing with Martha?" I asked him the next time we talked.

"Stella, will you please stay out of my social life?"

"I will, once you get it straightened out.

Roger, you just weren't put on Earth to run your own life. You're good at feeding white rats sugared water and that's it. Come on. What happened between you and Martha?"

"We went to the wedding and she had too much champagne and got sick in the car. When I brought her home, her daughter, who was in the living room, accused me of getting her mother drunk so I could assault her.

"I denied it and told Martha I didn't want to see her again because I can't stand women who can't hold their liquor. Martha called me a week later and asked me if I wanted to go to Bermuda with her. I told her I didn't think it was a good idea. And do you know what she said? 'You used me!' "

I apologized to Roger. "It doesn't sound like Martha and you were good for each other."

"She was about average."

Roger's Story

I'm in serious trouble. Stella found out from Prudin about my mortgaging the house and advancing the money to Twoey. I'm not sure how Prudin found out. They must occasionally allow a snitch into Heaven.

She was so furious she woke me up in the middle of the night and screamed, "How could you mortgage our house?"

I said, "It's not our house anymore, it's my house. Twoey will pay me back next month."

"Twoey's an idiot and now he's going to lose our house."

"I didn't mortgage the whole house. I refinanced it. The bank was happy to do it, and I can use the loan to invest in Apple computers."

"Why didn't you use my money to invest in Wall Street?"

"That money is too sacred, Stella, and I would never gamble with it. One of the main advantages of being a widower is that you find out what to put your money into and what's too great a risk. Twoey put up his houses in Hoboken to guarantee my loan, anyway. You're not supposed to worry about money while you are in Heaven."

"Don't tell me what I'm supposed to do in Heaven. I want you to pay our mortgage back with my insurance money."

I promised her I would, though God knows how.

Meanwhile, Mimi's on a buying rampage. She uses Saul's credit card whenever she wants something. Last week I asked her if that was fair and she replied, "He's loaded. Do you know how much optometrists make? More than orthodontists. They don't make much on the glasses but there's a hundred percent profit in the frames. People will spend anything to look good."

"Does it bother Saul that she uses his Visa

card?" Stella asked me.

"It doesn't seem to. Mimi tells him that since spending money makes her happy, it should make him happy. His kids don't like it a bit."

"I didn't know he had children."

"Mimi says he has three and they're all mad at her because they think Mimi is going to use up all of their inheritance, and they're probably right. Saul has never introduced Mimi to his kids because he's afraid of a nuclear explosion."

"Are his children married?"

"All three are and they have children too, so you can see what a threat Mimi is."

"I give her credit. At least she is doing something for her heart, which is more than I can say for you. Now tell me, does Mimi want you to get married?"

"She said she wouldn't mind my getting married as long as I didn't make the same mistake twice."

Stella's Story

There are worse things in the world than Mimi giving me one more dig after all I've done for her. There was a plane crash over Italy and suddenly 160 people showed up in our part of Heaven at the same time. Moses said we'd have to double up until he could find other housing for them. We were furious because if you have to share your room, you're no longer in the clouds.

They assigned a nun, Sister Linda from St. Louis, to share my room. The first thing she did was put a crucifix on the wall. The second thing she did was get on her knees and pray to it. After praying she asked, "Are you Catholic?"

"No," I said, "I'm Jewish."

"Our Lord is Jewish."

"I've heard that," I said. "How many times do you pray a day, anyway?"

"Four or five, whatever moves me. As soon as the engine on the plane caught on fire, I said, 'Dear Lord, make it fast and deliver me to your Heaven.' "

"Well, your prayers were answered."

"I feel bad for all the other people on board. No one survived. I think most of them are up here. Would you like to pray with me sometime?"

"I guess so. There can't be any harm in it since up here we all have the same God."

"Have you seen Jesus?" she asked me.

"No," I told her. "I don't know where he is."

"I'll find him. It's always been my mission. I know Jesus would never stay at the Ritz-Carlton. He's probably out in the desert with his disciples."

"Well, up here we all believe we have the same God. He's around somewhere."

Sister Linda then said, "I'm not sure I can go along with that until I talk to my bishop."

When Bea heard I was bunking with a nun she

came to visit. Sister Linda was very outgoing and funny and didn't seem to be disturbed when we asked a lot of questions.

She told us she came from a family of ten. She'd been a nun for twenty years and taught art at Our Lady of Victory High School in St. Louis. She'd won a free trip to Rome from the Knights of Columbus as the Teacher of the Year. The prize included an audience with the Pope. Sister Linda said it was the biggest moment of her life but she didn't expect that a plane crash and a trip to Heaven would be thrown in. She told us, it was God's decision, and He must have had a reason for it.

I told her that she was the first nun I had met close up and she admitted that she didn't know too many Jewish women in her business either.

Bea said, "Do you think we killed Christ?"

Sister Linda said, "I don't, but my brothers do. They heard it in parochial school."

Sister Linda wasn't much of a bother. She even sang after she found Elvis Presley's guitar in the music room. The only time she seemed unhappy was when she thought about all the other people who were killed on the plane with her. She said, "Suppose some of them didn't make it to Heaven? Everyone on the plane was different. There were business travelers, people from all over the world, college students."

Sister Linda shook her head.

"Why do you think God did it?"

"God can't be responsible for everything. It

could have been a pilot error or maybe the ground personnel forgot to put gas in the engine."

"I hadn't thought of that."

Once Sister Linda got into trouble because she was praying to God that Notre Dame would win its football game against the army. Connie Pollack's son had gone to West Point and she didn't like the idea of Linda praying for victory in South Bend. Connie complained to Moses and one night he came to our suite. He said, "We prefer it if you don't pray for football victories. There are many other things to pray for but God doesn't consider prayers on the gridiron."

Sister Linda felt chastised. "But all nuns pray for Notre Dame. It's part of our religion."

Moses said, "I can understand that but God can't choose between Notre Dame and another team."

I told her Moses usually didn't come down that hard on anyone.

Sister Linda said, "He probably knows someone at the University of Southern California."

The one problem I had with Sister Linda is that it was very difficult for me to talk to Roger when she was in the room.

One time she said, "You were talking in your sleep."

I told her the truth. "I wasn't talking in my sleep. I was talking to my husband, Roger, on Earth." Not surprised by this she said, "That's a nice thing to do. Does he talk to you?"

"Yes," I said. "All the time. We keep each other informed. Roger lives in the same house with his mother and our daughter, Sarah, and her baby. It's nice to still be close to them."

After Sister Linda moved in, my room was the most popular one in Heaven, especially when she sang for us. She knew folk songs and religious songs, and songs in French and Spanish. The most requested was "Amazing Grace." People were very quiet when she sang it and thought of the loved ones they had left behind.

One day Moses came by and told Sister Linda that he had found a place for her. It was a school for teenage angels run by the Sisters of Charity. Since there was no need for charity in Heaven we didn't know why the school existed. But Moses said they needed a good soccer coach.

Sister Linda left the next day and we were all sad. Bea said, "She was nice enough to be in a movie."

A few days later I was in the swimming pool and could not believe my eyes.

"Oh my God."

Bea said, "What's wrong?"

"Over there by the gazebo. It's Mimi!"

"It can't be. She's still alive, isn't she?"

Mimi, with a big grin on her face, waved and came over to the pool. She said, "Hi, Stella! Long time no see."

"What are you doing here?"

"Didn't Roger tell you? I dropped dead last night at dinner."

"How did you get here?"

"I choked on a piece of lobster shell at the No Bones About It Restaurant. Saul didn't know the Heimlich maneuver and neither did the employees. Roger has got a good suit on his hands. I'm finally going to make him rich."

"Mimi, there must be some mistake. You shouldn't have been sent here."

"Who says? Everyone eligible for Heaven can ask to go where he or she wants. I asked for the Ritz-Carlton. I could get used to this place."

She looked the hotel over.

At this moment St. Peter came out, took Mimi's bag and escorted her into the lobby. I got out of the pool, went to my bedroom and tried to contact Roger.

It took time because he was at the funeral home. Finally, two hours later he called me.

"Mimi's dead." Roger was sobbing.

"I know," I shouted at him. "She's up here with me. How could you do this to me?"

"Do what?"

"Why did you tell her where I was, knowing someday she would die and ask to go to the same place I did?"

"I didn't do it purposely. One night I was crying after talking to you and I confessed to her that we talked every day, and she asked where you were and I told her. I feel so terrible. She was such a beautiful mother and she didn't even like lobster."

"She came up here to drive me crazy."

"Stella, you forget Mimi always went where she wanted."

"How could I forget?"

"I just came back from the funeral home and made final arrangements. Sarah is beside herself with grief. Timmy feels just as bad and Gregory keeps crying. Mimi's being missed more than I thought."

"Are you going to give her a big funeral?"

"Not as big as yours. After all, you knew a lot more people. I don't believe any of the peaceniks ever knew her name."

"Well, she's ruined my day." I hung up.

Bea came into my room and saw how distraught I was. "We should go speak to Moses. He can send her somewhere else."

We found Moses hanging a Cézanne in the gym.

I asked, "What's my mother-in-law doing up here?"

Moses pretended innocence. "Who?"

"Mimi. How did she get up here?"

"She said you asked for her."

"That's a lie. The last person I would ask to join me in Heaven is my mother-in-law. You have to get rid of her."

"It's not that easy. All the paperwork has been done. I can't just send her off now after she has been assigned here. Our computer isn't programmed to do that."

"You can do anything."

"One of the rules of Heaven is you can't change things around just because you don't like them. You have to learn to make peace with each other. Otherwise you get sent to a Motel 6."

Bea said, "That's not a solution."

We stood firm.

Moses finally said, "We're going to have to take this to King Solomon."

He made an appointment for Mimi, Bea and myself to meet with King Solomon in the Royal Suite, which turned out to be a palatial penthouse with gold faucets and paintings by Goya, Renoir and Monet. Arthur Rubinstein was playing at the piano.

"This would be a nice room for me," Mimi said.

Moses ignored her and explained there was a mix-up in housing and the mother-in-law and the daughter-in-law were sent to the same place in Heaven, something everyone in management tries to avoid.

Solomon said, "Why can't you live together in Heaven?"

Mimi said, "I can, but she can't."

I said, "She lived with us on Earth and it wasn't any picnic. Why should she live with me in Heaven now?"

"Let me see the files."

St. Peter handed Solomon his notebook. After reading the record, the King raised his eyebrows and said, "I think we're playing with fire if both Folgers are permitted to stay in the same place.

141

What I suggest is Mimi goes to Palm Beach Breakers, which is only five miles away, and that she receive the same accommodations she was given here."

Mimi was furious. "I'm not moving. I will stay where I am. Let her move."

I yelled back, "I was here first."

Bea said, "Stella is staying right where she is."

Everyone was shocked to hear Mimi say she wouldn't do what King Solomon said she had to do. It was the first time I'd seen Moses upset. St. Peter's hand was shaking. Solomon was biting his lip. He said to Mimi, "Tomorrow, pack up and leave."

That afternoon we were taking a cooking lesson from Escoffier when Ronnie Sandler, one of our friends, came into the room and said, "You're not going to believe this. Mimi Folger is picketing Heaven. She's carrying a sign claiming God discriminates against mothers-in-law."

I looked at Bea and she looked at me and whispered, "Now at least they'll know why we don't want to live in the same place as she does."

When I looked out the window I could see angels running back and forth and Moses trying to talk Mimi out of picketing and not having any success.

The next time I saw Mimi was at dinner. She seemed quite happy about causing so much havoc. While I was very mad at her, I still wanted news of the family.

"What's really going on with Roger?" I asked.

"He doesn't think much of your plan to find him a wife. He doesn't think he needs one. As far as home life is concerned, he's very dependent on Miss Arnaud. She started making decisions for Gregory and now she's making decisions for him. He's very confused. Every woman he goes out with has a flaw. I offered to find someone to his liking but he turned me down. Twoey's women are practically jailbait and you're not helping him find a wife because you don't know what Roger likes. In fact, since I'm his mother, I want you to put me on the search committee."

I said to Bea right in front of Mimi, "I told you she would drive me up the wall."

Mimi said, "I think you should know while I was dying I made a request of Roger. I asked him to talk to me like he talks to you. He was crying at that moment and he agreed. Now there are two of us who can keep an eye on him."

She sat back and smiled, quite pleased with herself.

I left the table without eating the Cherries Jubilee. When I got to my room, I called Roger and asked, "Did you agree to talk to Mimi after you talked to me?"

"What could I do? She was dying and it was her last wish."

"The thorn in my marriage has followed me to Heaven."

"She feels I have a duty to speak to her. But I told her not to overdo it."

"So what happens when I talk to you and the line is busy?"

"I promise. I'll talk to her in the morning and you at night."

The next day St. Peter went up to get Mimi's bags. She hadn't packed and she said she wasn't leaving. She threatened to stage a sit-in in God's office if they tried to kick her out. Moses came to see me and asked me if there was any way I could talk Mimi into moving. I told him there was no way she would listen to me. I thought the only chance we might have is if he told Mimi that Saul was at the Palm Beach Breakers.

Moses said, "We've got to do something. God is furious and can't understand why anyone would cause trouble in Heaven. At the same time He can't afford to use force because word would get out that Heaven isn't what it's cracked up to be."

While we were talking St. Peter came in and told Moses that Mimi was sitting in the lobby of the Ritz with a large sign which read HELL NO, I WON'T GO.

All the residents were shaken when they saw her. The tranquillity of Heaven was threatened. If you can't have peace in paradise, where can you have it?

The worst thing was that everyone was mad at me. And these were the same people in the past who had told me they loved me.

I told Roger, "Your mother has turned all the residents against me."

Roger said, "What else is new?"

I found out from Mary Magdalene that management had decided not to force the issue. They assumed Mimi would tire of protesting and go quietly into the night. They didn't know Mimi. She locked herself in that night and slept on the floor.

When Mary Magdalene begged her to come out she said, "You're fooling with the person who threw rotten eggs at Henry Kissinger."

In the next few days Mimi was busy. She tried to organize the angels in the kitchen into a union. When someone pointed out they weren't paid Mimi said, "All the more then. Everyone needs better working conditions."

Hand-painted signs appeared on the elevators inviting people to attend "Free the Angels Day."

I'd never seen Mimi so happy. The more she angered all the other residents who were fearful God would become upset and kick everyone out, the more things she thought of to irritate them. God had finally met his match.

The next week I received a visit from Moses. He told me he was in the soup. He could not remove Mimi with force because force is never used in Heaven.

"What do you want from me?" I asked him.

"We want to let Mimi stay here."

"That's not fair."

"No, Stella, on Earth life is not fair."

"She'll drive me batty."

"You'll get used to it. Please, Stella, as a favor to me."

It's hard to refuse Moses when he asks a favor, particularly when you know he speaks for God. Reluctantly I said okay, which made Bea angry when she heard about it.

So Mimi was informed she could stay, which she considered a big victory considering the Heavenly forces that had been against her.

When I told Roger what happened, he just laughed.

Roger's Story

Things went screwy for a few days. Sarah's in mourning, and if it weren't for Samantha there would be no hope for me. But Samantha is getting mad because she said Sarah isn't helping her take care of Gregory enough. She's threatening to quit. She said I really was just like Yul Brynner in *The King and I* and that I only thought about myself.

I begged her to stay and promised everything in the house would change, though I really have no idea how I would make it happen.

To complicate my life, I'm still receiving sympathy visits over Mimi and because of them, I've lost a lot of time at the lab. Most of the people dropping by were members of her various protest groups and I didn't know any of them.

Stella said, "I guess you can't get romantically involved if you're so busy at home."

I assured her I couldn't. This was a lie because

I had gotten involved with someone, and I wasn't about to reveal who the person was because I was certain Stella would screw it up.

I was confused, though. How much should a late wife have to say about her husband's personal affairs? I took my problem to Rabbi Sparkman, who didn't bat an eye at the idea I was still in touch with Stella.

He said, "There is nothing in the Torah about the subject. Since it is not written in stone, Stella feels she can do anything she wants. If you were afraid of her on Earth, no wonder you're afraid of her now."

"So what do I do?"

"Nothing. It will all work out."

I shook his hand and said, "Thank you, Rabbi. You will go down in Jewish history as one of the great ones."

That week I also received a visit from B. B. Barnett, a lawyer for the Stardust Life and the lobster company. He said he was representing the restaurant where Mimi had "tragically passed away." Since Stardust never likes to go to court if they can avoid it, he was willing to discuss a reasonable settlement. The offer was $75,000, which he said was very generous for a woman Mimi's age. I called Twoey and in fifteen minutes he was at the house.

The Stardust man was nervous. "Did you know the deceased?" he asked Twoey.

"She was like a mother to me. She certainly was worth more than $75,000." Twoey looked at him like a basset hound needing his water bowl filled.

The man knew he was up against reinforced steel. "What do you think she was worth?"

Twoey was ready to drink greedily.

"If we went to court probably a million. But we're reasonable. Give us $150,000 and we'll forget your negligence."

The two arrived at $100,000 and the insurance man said the check would be in the mail in the next few weeks.

When he left Twoey said, "Now we can go back to building houses. I'm looking at a piece of land in Astoria not too far from LaGuardia Airport. We'll also take some of the money and pay off a part of your mortgage."

"Twoey, this was my mother. Are you sure she would have wanted to be invested in Astoria?"

"Your mother always loved Astoria. It's the next Las Vegas."

Stella's Story

Mimi is on my back all the time. She arranged to have her padded lounge chair next to mine and she joins us for meals at our table.

Roger is the main subject of conversation, of course. He told Mimi that she had a very nice funeral with twenty Vietnam War protesters from Queens and Brooklyn that Sarah invited. Rabbi

Sparkman had nothing much to say but Timothy Leary, who'd never met Mimi, gave an inspiring eulogy.

Channel Five was there and so were reporters from the *Daily News* and the *New Republic*. The *New York Post* said it would have sent someone but they had to cover a freak infestation of fleas in Brooklyn. The service was arranged by the Socialist Party of Queens Village who likened Mimi to Emma Goldman and told the press Mimi was one of the heroines of the American labor movement.

Our table listened with mixed feelings. Mimi was still determined to change the system in Heaven although no one else thought there was anything wrong with it.

To make me miserable she insisted that she choose the next candidate for Roger since the rest of us were so unsuccessful. Bea told her if she had a say in the search she would resign.

Mimi said, "Big deal. You don't even know my son. Why should you choose a new wife for him anyway?"

I reminded both of them that people would think it was in bad taste for Roger to date so soon after his mother died.

Mimi disagreed. "He's getting a lot of sympathy so we should strike while the iron is hot. You always get a man to marry someone when he's at his weakest."

Bea concurred, to a point. "From what you tell us, Stella, Roger is at his wit's end. He won't put up any resistance if he can find a woman who will make him happier."

"So what do we do now? Mimi, you were last to see Roger. Did you notice if Roger was attracted to any particular type of woman?"

"He didn't mention it. Of course, I was there, so why would he need another woman?"

I looked at Bea and she at me.

Mimi sighed and said, "But now that I'm no longer there I think we should find someone for him."

I said, "Roger doesn't like to be bothered with too many details so he has to find someone to take the household worries off his shoulders."

"You would think we would have come up with somebody by now," Bea said. "There are millions of women out there looking for a man."

Bea threw out a few more candidates and so did Mimi and so did I. Some lived too far away and we couldn't figure out how Roger would meet them. Others had major flaws such as acute arthritis and high blood pressure. We all agreed that Roger deserved a healthy second wife so he would not lose her soon after marrying her.

Henrietta Dubinsky was fifty-five and had never married, so it was decided she would make a lousy grandmother for Gregory. Liz Himmelfarb was too High Maintenance and Marisa Starr, a friend of Bea's, kept getting speeding tickets and would probably lose her license any day now.

Roger's Story

Stella complained that she didn't like my lifestyle.

"I don't know what my lifestyle has to do with you. I'm enjoying the life of a single person. I have it all except I worry about Sarah and Gregory. Do you know where Sarah takes your grandchild every night? The Hard Rock Dairy and Disco. Do you think that's a place to take a baby?"

"I thought you had a nurse."

"Miss Arnaud. She leaves at six o'clock when Sarah comes home from pottery school."

"I didn't know Sarah was in pottery school."

"She enrolled because she thought she needed a profession. Her first choice was real estate and her second was pottery. But real estate bored her because the buyers only protested one thing: the price. Maybe I'll get married just to have someone take care of Gregory."

Stella's Story

To solve Roger's problem we formed a committee made up of Bea, Mimi, me, Eleanor Crouse and Sophie Dartmouth. Eleanor had lived in Nassau County and Sophie came from White Plains, so those two regions were covered. Several women would have loved to be on the committee but we wanted to keep it small so there were no fights.

We held our meetings in the Vienna Café because the pastries in Heaven are out of this world. I opened the meeting by saying, "Roger is ripe for a wife. He doesn't know what to do with Gregory when Miss Arnaud leaves at six. If we can come up with a candidate, he'll definitely accept her."

Sophie said, "I wonder if there's someone in my old yoga class he might go for."

Eleanor said, "There is a lady I used to play Scrabble with. But she was married three times."

"We owe it to Roger to find him someone who's only been married one or two times," I said. "We want him to be happy."

"He didn't seem that happy when he was with you," Mimi said.

I ignored that one and reached for a piece of ruggeleh.

"Wait a minute!" Mimi cried. "I just thought of someone! She's a New York City police-woman."

I said, "What does she look like?"

"Angie Dickinson, I swear. She's been cited for bravery twice by the Mayor. She has never been married but she has a great bosom. Every time someone tries to touch her there she arrests them."

Bea said, "How do you know her?"

"She arrested me once for disturbing the peace at City Hall. Her name is Frieda Mindlin and she lives in Kew Gardens."

The strategy was to have Frieda arrest Roger

for illegal parking. Then she would start talking with him as a human being.

"But how will that get them together?" Sophie asked.

Mimi said, "She's always in heat. I think she gets turned on by her own uniform. She'll do all the work. Just think, Roger will be the talk of Forest Hills. He will go into New York and no one will fool with him. She's trained in the martial arts so she'll be the perfect mother for Gregory, and if Sarah ever gets arrested again she'll be able to get her out."

"Won't she have lousy hours?"

"If her schedule doesn't work out maybe she'll quit. Our only problem is to get Roger to park illegally on the beat where she works."

I told Roger that a few years ago I had left a little black dress to be cleaned at the Elite Cleaners, and they probably just hadn't had the heart to bring it to Roger. Now that Sarah was bigger, I was sure she could fit in it. I knew you could never get a parking place near the cleaners and he would have to double park. Mimi told us Frieda drove by there every fifteen minutes.

The idea of having a policewoman in the family intrigued me nearly as much as it did Mimi and Bea. First of all, she would have fantastic stories to tell at night, and as a New York cop she would scare bad people away from the house.

We waited to hear from Roger, while Mimi caused more havoc in Heaven. She wanted television, something we were all against. She said,

"This can't be Heaven if you can't watch *Wheel of Fortune*."

I waited for a week before asking Roger for a report on Frieda. He sounded really down.

"You're not going to believe this but I took a policewoman out to dinner. It was the only way I could avoid a ticket."

"Was she nice?"

"Yes."

"So, do I hear wedding bells?"

"No."

"Why not?"

"She likes girls."

"Oh my God," I said. "Are you sure?"

"Stella, she told me she likes girls, but prefers to arrest men. I've had it with the women I keep going out with. Dating is a jungle."

"I hope you don't think I set this up."

Roger was quiet for a while, then said, "Look, we ought to take some time out. This doesn't mean anything has changed between us. It's just that life has to go on and I feel you're trying to interfere in any future plans I might make. So I'm going to take a breather."

The girls and Mimi were shocked when I reported the conversation. Mimi said, "And Frieda is a public figure and got accolades from the Mayor. You could have fooled me."

For three weeks I tried to get Roger on the phone but he wasn't answering. I could only gather he was much madder at me about the policewoman than I had thought. Finally he called to give me some news.

Sarah was dating. Roger said that wasn't the news. The news was that her boyfriend worked for Goldman Sachs, and he had come to the house in a Calvin Klein pin-striped suit and a blue shirt and striped tie. He said weird things like "please" and "thank you" and got a big kick out of reading to Gregory.

Mimi was shocked and said, "I bet he even reads *The Wall Street Journal*."

Bea said, "This sounds pretty good. If Sarah doesn't blow it, Gregory will wind up with a father after all."

In fact, a few weeks later Roger told me, "Dennis Robinson the Third wants to marry Sarah."

"How do you know?"

"He came to me yesterday to ask permission."

"Where is he from?"

"Greenwich, Connecticut."

"Is he Jewish?"

"I don't think so. But I'm sure Sarah can convert him."

"Well, at least we don't have to worry about her winding up with a taxi driver. Besides, you'll save money. You won't have to pay a nanny to take care of Gregory."

There was a pause on the other end and finally Roger said, "Miss Arnaud is going to stay."

"Why?"

"I'm going to marry her."

No one faints in Heaven or I would have.

"Why, Roger, why?"

"I'm in love with her and I know she loves all of us. Besides, she knows where all the pots and pans and fuse boxes are, so I won't have to break her in."

"Very funny. But how do you know she's right for you?"

"It doesn't matter. I would never be happy if someone else picked out a wife for me. Miss Arnaud is the best of the litter."

"Stop calling her Miss Arnaud!" I yelled. "If you're in love with her, you can at least call her by her first name."

"Okay. Samantha, then."

"That's a dumb name for a second wife."

"What it means is that it's now difficult for us to talk. Samantha heard us when she was taking care of Gregory and she said she wouldn't marry me if I kept conversing with you. She said the time has come for me to deal with the fact that you are gone forever."

"Besides being a nanny, now she's a psychiatrist?"

"You see, Stella, it would never work. You can't interfere in my life after I'm married. No woman would stand for it."

I couldn't take it anymore. I hung up and went to see Moses and told him what had happened.

He told me, "You should have expected it, Stella. What did you think would happen to Roger?"

"I don't even know the lady. She could be a

gold-digger or a Scientologist."

"Stella, the toughest thing to do is to cut your ties. You had to when you came up here but because you loved Roger so and he loved you, it has taken time. Life on Earth must continue and you will only disrupt the natural order of things if you get involved."

"Well, I want to go to the wedding. I know it's a big favor, but I want to go with Bea and Mimi. Please?"

That threw Moses for a loop.

"I can't do that. It's never been done. Once you're here, you can't go back."

"Moses, you can do anything."

Moses stood firm.

"All right, I'll use up my third wish. My wish is to go to the wedding."

"This will have to go higher up."

Roger told me that the wedding would be in a month. He said he didn't want to make it a big deal. He was afraid that if our old friends attended they would not be nice to Samantha.

Samantha's friends, he said, were excited because she'd never been married before. She had gone from one baby to the next and, until Roger, she never believed there'd be a man in her life.

Bea and Mimi and I discussed it.

Since Samantha was not a divorcée or a widow, we agreed she had no experience with men. She was probably good at making sure Roger's life was in order, but she had no knowledge about what she should do to keep Roger in line, which every man needs if the marriage is to survive.

Mimi was put out that Roger had not consulted her. I was mad because he fell in love behind my back.

There was talk of boycotting the wedding, but all three of us thought that was a dumb idea.

Finally word was passed from Moses. "King Solomon says you can attend the wedding, but you cannot talk to anyone and you will not be seen. This permission is unprecedented, so if you mess up, you can't come back here."

I told Bea and Mimi, and then Bea said, "What should we wear?"

"It's summertime down there, so we should wear something flowery and made of silk."

Mimi said, "We could have a famous dress designer come up with something smashing."

I said, "I love white shoes. I hope they'll go with my outfit."

Bea said, "And hats. I want one of those big straw hats that women wear to the Kentucky Derby."

We went to Christian Dior and told him what the occasion was and what our requirements were. We also told him it was a rush job.

He designed a peach organdy dress for Bea, a white strapless dress for Mimi, and for me a tan suit with pearl buttons, just like the one he made for Jackie Kennedy. We all regretted that no one down there would see us, but it still made us feel good that we had something nice to wear to Roger's wedding.

Roger and I were still talking. He told me that he and Samantha were going to Hawaii for their honeymoon. When they came back she wanted to redecorate the house.

I said, "What's the matter with the house? Now she doesn't like my taste?"

"It's nothing against you. But she wants her own house with her own furniture. She said she is going to be my wife and she doesn't want me to forget it. She said I can still have one eight-by-ten photograph up of you on the mantel but that's it. Samantha has a mind of her own. I hadn't realized how strong-willed she was until she said, 'I want my own plants and not somebody else's.' "

I didn't know what was wrong with my plants. I decided to change the subject. "So who's coming to the wedding?"

"Just family. Samantha has a sister in Canada and her mother lives in Sun City, Arizona. I'm bringing some friends from the lab, and Sarah has invited a few of her friends. Timmy felt if he invited anyone it would be disloyal to you."

"Are you going to be married by Rabbi Sparkman?"

"The rabbi and a Unitarian minister will be on standby. I'm having the Kew Gardens Deli cater it. I wish you could be here."

"What exactly does that mean? If I were there you wouldn't be getting married."

"I forgot that."

"Is she any good in bed?"

I could tell Roger was angry. "It's none of your business and the answer to your question is we have not slept together. For all I know, she's a virgin. But you're not going to get information like that out of me. Good night."

Bea and Mimi laughed when they heard the conversation. "Well, at least Roger wasn't talked into marrying because Samantha used her wiles as a negotiating point," Bea said.

Mimi said, "Roger was never someone who would make the first move. He is not a lady's man, though he could have been if he'd wanted to."

I had little contact with Roger before the wedding. Finally on the big day St. Peter flew us down in the Heavenly Helicopter. The three of us looked gorgeous and as we left the Ritz everyone was standing on the lawn, complimenting us. They didn't know where we were going but they might have guessed. Mrs. Jacobson said as she kissed me, "I don't want to go back but it would be nice to see the old place again."

When we got to the temple St. Peter took us to the choir loft, where we could look down on everyone.

The crowd was small. Rabbi Sparkman and the Unitarian minister were standing up front. I saw Timmy, who was Roger's best man, standing next to them. Samantha was being given away by a man I didn't know who turned out to be her brother. Sarah was standing there holding Gregory, the cutest grandson that ever lived, and next to her was a man in a double-breasted, navy blue Armani blazer, whom I assumed was Dennis.

The three of us concentrated on Samantha.

"She's too thin," Bea said. "There's nothing for Roger to hold on to when they're making love."

"No bosom," I declared. "Why would Roger marry someone with no breasts?"

Mimi, who was the only one who had actually seen her, said, "I've seen her in the shower. She does have a nice bosom. Her problem is she wears shapeless bras so people don't know it."

I could tell Roger was nervous. He kept playing with his car keys. Someone struck up the organ and the ceremony began. Suddenly Gregory started to wail. He didn't like what was going on at all. The wail turned into a scream. He kept reaching out for Samantha. She stopped walking down the aisle and took Gregory in her arms. He immediately became quiet. And that's how the couple were married, the two of them with Baby Gregory, standing in front of the rabbi and the Unitarian minister. It was a lovely scene and after they were pronounced man and wife, Bea, Mimi and I were crying our hearts out. Then something unexpected happened.

Sarah went up to our rabbi and they had a discussion. The rabbi was arguing and finally nodded his head. Sarah signaled Dennis to come up to the altar. Then it dawned on us she wanted Rabbi Sparkman to marry them. Roger and Samantha, still holding Gregory, turned to witness this.

"It's a miracle!" I said.

All Mimi said was, "It's a miracle he converted."

Bea said, "He seems like a nice boy but a bit stiff."

Mimi said, "He may be stiff but he makes $300,000 a year, not counting bonuses. Sarah could do a lot worse."

The rabbi married them in five minutes and the three of us were crying again. We had expected one celebration, not two.

The helicopter came down after the ceremony and took us back to Heaven. I was happy and sad at the same time. Bea assured me that Roger's second marriage would have a 50–50 chance of succeeding.

Roger's Story

I've never been so frightened in my life, not even when I married Stella. I was taking a new trip with a woman who was almost a stranger.

After what happened with the rabbi, I asked Samantha if she had any problem with our age difference. Over the bread she was kneading (she

162

actually makes bread), she grinned and said, "What? You mean like when I was in elementary school you were in college?"

I knew then that the difference would only be a good source of humor in our lives.

I hadn't liked being a widower and at the same time I wasn't sure I could handle another wife. If you're wondering, I do love Samantha. And both of us know Stella will always be somewhere in the background.

I have to say, being with Samantha was strange at first. She worked for me and now she was in charge of me. At least I have someone to tell me what to do now. I know I love her. Not the way I had loved Stella for so many years, but Samantha is something new in my life. And she gives me a center.

One of the things that came out of the wedding is that Twoey talked Dennis into investing in his houses in Astoria. He said he would take the money from Dennis and pay back Stella's insurance funds to me. This made Dennis not only my son-in-law but also my business partner, and I could now get the house out of mortgage.

Samantha, who saw everything that went on, told Twoey that he was not to introduce me to any blonde women, single, married, divorced or what have you. The policewoman could remain my friend, but not the others. She said she admired Twoey, but his lifestyle was and always would be different than mine. When I witnessed this conversation, I kept my mouth shut. Twoey promised her that the only thing he would discuss with me is how to build a barbecue pit.

Stella's Story

I was in my bedroom, hanging up my dress, when Roger called.

"Stella, I've called to say goodbye."

I was dumbfounded. "Why 'goodbye'?"

"I have a new life and it doesn't make any sense to keep up our communication. I will always love you and remember you, but you're part of my past now. If it helps you to hear it, I will miss you very much."

I didn't know what to say. I knew that what he was saying was the only way things could be, but I wasn't prepared for it.

"Maybe I could solve problems that are too much for you."

"No, Stella, it won't work. It would mess up my marriage with Samantha. You and I know we love each other. That's got to be enough now."

I thought it over while Roger breathed into the phone, waiting for some kind of response.

Maybe he was right. We loved each other still. Things were just different now.

I exhaled.

"I know you have to go on with your life, Roger. Maybe this way I can get on with things in Heaven. And maybe someday — not for a long time, of course — but maybe someday, I'll see you up here."

I managed to choke out, "And Samantha too."

As soon as we hung up I started to cry, something you're not supposed to do in Heaven.